"Is Max Adamms your boyfriend?" asked my little brother, Matthew.

"No. Not really."

"Well . . . are you in love with him?"

I had all the symptoms. I thought about him during class. I read every word in the fan magazines that I could get my hands on. And now I had his picture up on my wall. Still, it didn't feel like true love.

I stared Max right in the eye. He peered back, not moving a muscle. It was a very one-sided relationship.

The Victoria Mahoney Series
by Shelly Nielsen
    Just Victoria
    More Victoria
    Take a Bow, Victoria
    Only Kidding, Victoria
    Maybe It's Love, Victoria
    Autograph, Please, Victoria
    Who's Your Hero, Victoria?
    Then and Now, Victoria

A White Horse Book
Published by Chariot Books™,
an imprint of David C. Cook Publishing Co.
David C. Cook Publishing Co., Elgin, Illinois 60120
David C. Cook Publishing Co., Weston, Ontario

WHO'S YOUR HERO, VICTORIA?
© 1989 by Shelly Nielsen

Cover illustration by Gail Roth
First printing, 1989
Printed in the United States of America
93 92 91 90 90   ' 2 3 4 5

Library of Congress Cataloging-in-Publication Data

Nielsen, Shelly, 1958—
   Who's your hero, Victoria? / Shelly Nielsen.
      p.   cm.—(The Victoria Mahoney series: #7) (A White horse
book)
   Summary: Feeling left out when her friends fall madly in love
with a young television star, thirteen-year-old Vickie turns to God
during a difficult time.
   ISBN 1-55513-626-6
   [1. Christian life—Fiction.] I. Title. II. Series: Nielsen.
Shelly, 1958- Victoria Mahoney series: #7.
PZ7.N5682Wh   1989
[Fic]—dc19   89-30058
                                                          CIP
                                                          AC

for LoraBeth,
editor and friend

1

On New Year's Eve, the sports store was packed, and the after-Christmas crowd was in a rotten mood. Come to think of it, I wasn't in such a hot mood, either. Under my winter coat, I was starting to sweat. And my arms hurt. Maybe the bad mood of the store was catching.

"I was here *first*," whined a little boy to the man cutting in front of him.

"Hey, do you *mind*?" said a white-haired woman when her toes got stepped on by another shopper.

The man waiting ahead of me said, "Could we pick up the service a *little*?"

I shifted the skis to my other arm. Dad and I were next in line. The clerk behind the counter looked as

7

if she'd bite off the head of the first customer who crossed her.

"Most kids get their Christmas gifts under the tree," I muttered, just loud enough for Dad to hear. "They don't have to stand in line for them."

My father looked down at me. He had an armload of boots, socks, poles, and special ski wax. The poles stuck out at sharp angles. He had already poked two shoppers, and he looked a little frazzled, like he does Saturday mornings after a hard Friday night of chef-ing at the restaurant.

"Don't be such an ingrate. You know your mother and I can't afford to outfit you in skis at full price. We thought our plan was pretty imaginative."

Mom and Dad had cut a photograph of cross-country skis from a newspaper flyer, put it in a shoebox, and wrapped it up like a regular present with a note that said, "All yours—during the after-Christmas sales!" At the time, I was pretty excited. But after-Christmas sales were a pain. And vacation was almost over—too late to get any real use out of skis. One more day of freedom, then I'd be back in school. Ugh.

I feel rotten, I thought with satisfaction. *Totally, absolutely, miserably rotten.*

Scowling, I saw a familiar face grinning at me across the store. My brain clicked and I realized that it was Mattie Baker from church. She waved from the weight-lifting department and yelled, "Hoo, there! Mahoneys! Hello!" so cheerfully that

8

everyone in the place turned to stare. She dropped the dumbbells she had been looking at and came marching over.

Mattie is a friend from way back who was my choir director when I was three. She is the zippiest person I know. Dad says, "Mattie Baker is incapable of forming a frown"—only a slight exaggeration.

"You're looking good," Dad said to her, juggling equipment so he could shake her hand.

"Yeah, I'm improving," she said. "And look." She brushed her hand over her head. "Growth. What do you think, Vickie? Is this new 'do' me?"

Her hair was blonde baby fuzz, no more than a half-inch long.

"It's you," I said.

I remembered the Sunday night service over a year ago when she had climbed the platform stairs and stood at the podium. "I have an announcement to make," she said in a tiny voice that echoed over the P.A. "I have just found out I have a disease called leukemia. Cancer." The congregation didn't make a move. Not one pew creaked.

Lately, she'd been having special treatments which made her throw up and her hair fall out. Somehow, she managed to keep this smiling attitude about stuff—even bad stuff. I don't know how. Not that she didn't get sad or frustrated at times, too. I mean, as the choir director of hyper little three- and four-year-olds, she was bound to get a little tense now and then. But mostly she had this grin that she

9

could switch on like a light bulb.

"Whose skis?" she asked, touching the shiny poles.

"Mine," I said. "My Christmas present."

"Lucky duck. All I got for Christmas was bubble bath." She winked to show she was kidding.

The clerk shoved a plastic bag across the counter to the man ahead of us. "Next!" she barked.

Dad and I piled our stuff on the counter.

"Will you two excuse me?" Mattie asked as the clerk searched out codes and numbers on the register. "I've got to go choose the dumbbells just right for me. But, hey, good luck with those skis, Vickie. See you on the slopes."

"So long, Mattie," my father said. "Take care."

After she was well out of earshot, he said to me, "Wow. Talk about an inspiration. Mattie Baker's got enough energy for you and me both, huh?"

When you're crabby the last thing you want is to bump into someone cheerful. "Hmmph," I said, and let myself droop back into my old grumpy, post-Christmas mood. People like Mattie weren't normal. They had some unusual knack for looking on the bright side. "If she had to go back to school day after tomorrow," I muttered, "she wouldn't be such a bucket of cheer."

"Yikes," he said as the clerk ripped the receipt off the register and started to bag our purchases. "Merry Christmas to you, Mr. Scrooge."

"Ho, ho, ho," I answered, baring my teeth in what hardly resembled a smile.

10

2

By the time Dad and I got home, it was snowing again. Mom came out to meet us on the front steps. The snowflakes in her dark hair sparkled like glitter.

"Did you get them?" she asked. "You did? Fantastic. Let's see." She was more excited than I was, which was a trick and a half.

"And we got the deal of a lifetime," my father told her as we lugged equipment into the living room. "It almost killed us, but it was worth it. Bobbi, I had no idea after-Christmas shoppers were so cutthroat. They're piranhas."

"Why do you think I wouldn't go with you?" Mom asked. "After Christmas, I don't leave this house until February. I'm no fool."

"Traitor," said Dad, but he smiled.

My brother, Matthew, came racing down the stairs. He is six years old, one of those little kids with missing teeth who looks more innocent than he really is. "Did you bring me anything?"

"No," I said. "So settle down."

He stopped like someone had tossed a bucket of ice water over him. "I was just asking, Crabbo."

Instantly he was revving up his engines again. "See what I've got, Vickie." He held up a kids' book. "It's about Eleanor Roosevelt. I checked it out of the library." He flopped down on the floor and started paging madly through the book. "Mom read it to me. Know what? Eleanor's mom called her 'Granny' 'cause when Eleanor was little she was sort of serious, like an old lady. That wasn't nice. Her dad never called her that. *He* called her 'my darling Nell.'" Suddenly Matthew yanked his head around and looked at the equipment spread all over the floor. "What's all this stuff?"

Sometimes you have to spell out the obvious to my little brother. "They're skis," I said.

My dad explained to Mom how you've got to wax cross-country skis to keep them slippery. It was old hat to me. A friend had taught me the finer points already. Maybe I'd give Peter a call later. See if he wanted to hit the old snowdrifts. On second thought, maybe I'd practice first.

"How about a demo?" Matthew asked. He jumped between the skis, which were lying parallel in the carpeting. He bent his knees, swung his arms, and made whooshing noises like he was whizzing down a Swiss slope. "How'm I doing?" he shouted.

"Perfect," I said, "if these were downhill skis. But it just so happens that they're cross-country skis. Totally different story."

He straightened up. "Oh."

"Maybe you'd better give us a real live demonstration, Vickie," Dad suggested. "Take 'em for a spin."

"That's a great idea," I agreed. "I'll go see Chels." I started out of the room, then ran back to give my parents surprise hugs.

"Thanks tons for the skis," I told them. "They're what I always wanted." Then I dashed upstairs to my room for a quick change.

Minnesota winter was huffing and puffing outside, so I layered up in long underwear and windbreakers under my parka. Downstairs I yanked on my mittens and swung a scarf around my neck. *Dashing,* I thought, looking in the hall mirror. (Except my bangs desperately needed a trim.)

Just one more tiny detail. I went to the kitchen and fished around in the junk drawer. Ah, there it was. The Walkman. With the earphones on, I slipped it into my coat pocket and jammed a hat over my head. I was ready to go.

Those skis made the neighborhood skim past. The snow whispered "shh, shh" under my feet. I was really moving. Big snowflakes pelted my face like wet kisses, and people out shoveling their driveways stopped to watch me slush past. Cross-country is hard work, but—in another way—so graceful you feel like you're flying.

Then I realized I hadn't tuned in my station. I snapped on the radio. (Not an easy trick, because my thick mittens made my hands like giant paws.) I skimmed the stations, and after a lot of scratchy static and one really loud station, I found it.

Every weekday, from two until four, my favorite talk show was on. It was called "Ask Angie Anything." Mostly, I missed the show because I was in school, but sometimes I caught the last hour or so. The host, Dr. Angela Airhart, gave advice to people who called in with problems. She had a sort of gravelly voice and always sounded very sympathetic and kind, like she understood exactly what they were going through. She said "hmm" a lot.

Sometimes the questions were real stumpers. For instance, one lady's husband was such a slob she couldn't stand to eat dinner with him. Once, she said, he even picked up his plate and licked it.

I wouldn't have thought up an answer in a million years. But Dr. Angie told her to try positive reinforcement, like you would with a kid. ("Honey, I love it when you use a napkin to wipe your mouth instead of using the tablecloth.") It was good advice, all right. The lady called back a couple of days later and said things were definitely improving. Her husband now ate his peas with a fork instead of with his fingers.

14

I had a picture in my mind of what Dr. Angie must look like. She'd wear a white doctor's smock. She'd be plump, with just enough wrinkles to make her look wise. She probably had extremely soft hands and little half-moon glasses. Maybe she pulled her hair back in a soft bun.

Now some guy was going at his question full-steam. "Dr. Airhart, I'm at my wits' end. What would *you* do about a son who wants to dye his hair lavender?"

I would never call a radio station for advice, mainly because my problems are all too embarrassing. Like, when was my body going to stop looking like I was ten instead of thirteen? I would rather die than say that on the air. But it was interesting to hear other people's problems. Dad said it was a little like eavesdropping, but I thought it was nice to know that someone was there to listen to you if you got really desperate.

I was nearly to Chelsie's. I hadn't told her I was coming; if you're best friends with someone, you don't have to call her up and plan things out. You just pop in and announce, "Ta-da, I'm here." And she'll say, "Good. Come on in and have some cocoa." Or "I was just thinking about you." Or "What took you so long?" That's the kind of friend Chels is.

I swished up her driveway, noticing a lot of fresh foot tracks in the snow leading to her house. *What's up?* I wondered.

Chelsie stuck her head out the door. "I just tried to call you. Your dad said you were on your way over. Get in here, pronto!" She disappeared again.

I unlatched myself from the skis and thunked the snow off my boots. Then I let myself into the house. Inside it felt cheerful and warm. I heard familiar voices in the kitchen.

The room was noisy with laughter. My friends Kristie, Janell, Peggy, and Chels were all lumped around the kitchen table, their heads bent over an open magazine. Everyone was talking at once.

"Hey-ya, kiddo," Peggy Hiltshire said as I pulled up a chair. "That's what Max always says. 'Hey-ya, kiddo.' "

I stared at her. "Who is Max?"

They looked at each other as if I had just said something very stupid. Eyes rolled.

Janell was the first to blurt out, "You don't know who Max is?" She crossed her arms and shook her brown hair. Her earrings clanked. "She doesn't know who Max is." Clank, clank.

"I heard, but I don't believe," said Kristie.

Finally Chelsie had pity on me. "Max Adamms," she said, "is from the TV show 'For Goodness' Sake' which runs Tuesday nights." She slid the magazine around so I could see for myself. "Max Adamms," she repeated.

The picture was a full-color shot of a guy standing by a swimming pool in jeans and a rumpled shirt. He was squinting. Next to the picture the headline screamed: "Are You His Dream Date?!" Max's arms were crossed, and he had a smile plastered on his face. It was the biggest, whitest smile I'd ever seen.

"He is kind of cute," I said.

"Kind of cute! Kind of cute!" shouted Kristie, falling back against her chair. "Max Adamms is more than cute. He's talented. He's smart. He's"—she drew a breath—"*gorgeous!*"

Chelsie giggled. "Kristie is kind of a big fan."

"His biggest fan," Kristie corrected her. "Look, Vickie." She held a T-shirt up against her chest. "I got this for Christmas." Behind the gigantic T-shirt, Kris—who is small and blonde—looked slightly hilarious. All five of us could have fit inside that shirt, but I knew better than to say so. Instead I read the huge, hot pink letters out loud: "Max Adamms for President."

"And I bought this magazine," Janell said. "Take a look and weep." It was called *Teen Fan,* and the cover was a mess of color photographs. Every headline was followed by about a thousand exclamation points.

Suddenly Peggy let out a piercing shriek. Kristie jumped in her chair and Janell, who hates surprises, scowled.

"What?" Chelsie said. "Speak up! Don't keep us in suspense!"

Peg looked red in the face. Janell pounded her on the back. "Are you all right? Did you swallow your tongue? Should we call an ambulance?"

Peg clapped her hand to her chest. "I have a brilliant idea."

We all leaned close.

"Let's start a Max Adamms fan club!"

There was a stunned moment of silence. Then everyone said, "Yeah! Fun. Let's do it!"

I was a little confused, like I'd just been spun in a circle and my head wasn't really clear yet. I had hardly realized that old Max Adamms existed before today. I peered again at his picture. He did have a nice smile.

There was a big flurry about who would get to be president of the club.

"How should we choose?" Peg asked. "We'd all make good presidents."

"I don't want to do it," I said. Again, I got very funny looks. "You guys know Max better."

"She's right," said Kristie. "That leaves us."

Janell said, "I need to know what the responsibilities would be. I have band practice every Thursday after school. My schedule is already packed."

"The president," said Chels, "gets to call the meetings. She coordinates the official fan club newsletter—"

"*What* newsletter?" said Janell.

Chels continued as if she hadn't heard a word. "—And if Max ever comes to town, she gets to represent the membership—meet him, talk to him, that sort of thing."

That last one was a doozy of a duty. The idea of actually *meeting* Max was too much. Kris, Peg, and Janell looked as though they'd just gotten socked in the gut.

Chelsie got up, opened a drawer, and pulled out a scrap of paper and a pencil stub.

"There's only one way to decide this. We have to do it democratically. We have to vote."

"Wait a second." I looked around the table. Their eager faces had identical, hopeful smiles. "You'll all vote for yourselves. I'll be the only tie breaker."

"That's the idea, old buddy, old pal," said Chelsie, fluttering her eyelashes and laying her head on my shoulder.

"That's not fair. The ones I don't pick will hate my guts."

Their faces drooped.

"She's right," Kristie said. "There's no telling what I might do if I don't win."

"I have an idea," Peggy said.

"Another idea?" Janell asked.

"Let's have a trivia contest. Vickie can make up questions from the magazine articles. We'll answer them. The last person to get stumped will be the official Max Adamms Fan Club president."

They gave me a few minutes to write down ideas. Then I started shooting out questions.

"You first, Peg," I said.

"I'm so nervous." She bit on her lip, pretending to be tense. "Okay, I'm ready. Shoot."

19

"Where was Max Adamms born?"

"Long Island, New York," she said. "Whew! That was close."

I turned to Janell.

"Age, hair color, and weight."

"Fourteen, black, one hundred and fifteen."

"Does he have a favorite food?"

"Of course." Chelsie blew on her fingernails and shined them on her shirt. "Vegetarian eggrolls."

"Ooo," said Kristie. "You're good."

"Elementary, my dear Watson," Chels said, grinning.

I turned to Kristie.

"What's his TV sister's name?"

"Easy," she said. "It's Alyssa." She looked at me. "She's really cute. Don't you love the way she wears her hair?"

Now I was back to Peggy. I searched the article for a stumper question. If I didn't come up with one soon, this quiz would last the rest of the day, with everyone getting correct answers.

"All right," I said. "Here's a good one. What's Max's favorite saying?"

There was a pause.

"Arrgh!" said Peggy. "That's a killer! I don't have the foggiest. How about 'Que sera, sera'?"

I made a buzzer noise like they have on TV game shows. "I'm sorry, contestant number 1. That answer is incorrect. Contestant number 2?"

Janell screwed up her face. "How about, 'When

the going gets tough, the tough get going'?"

"Nope. Chels?"

"I'm not even going to guess. Max is cute and everything, but I'm not a walking dictionary of information about him. What do you think I am, some sort of fanatic?"

"That leaves it up to you, Kris," I said. "If you can answer the million dollar question, you win the contest."

Kristie pulled herself up very tall. "I'll tell you what his favorite saying is. It's 'No nukes!' "

Janell whistled. "You're good!"

I shook Kristie's hand. "I crown you queen of the Max Adamms fan club."

"That's president," Chels corrected me.

But Kristie didn't notice. She was too busy being royal. She bowed to us and said "Thank you, thank you" in an English accent. Then she straightened up and went back to her regular old voice. "As my first official act of my queenship, I declare a raid on the refrigerator. I'm starved."

3

It was already getting dark when I suited up, strapped on my skis, waved to my friends, and headed for home. I whipped along at sixty miles per hour.

The house smelled delicious. *Spaghetti*, I thought, sniffing. With Dad's famous tomato sauce. And garlic toast—heavy on the garlic.

Dad came out to the living room, wiping his hands on his apron. "There you are. I'm making a New Year's Eve dinner and I need you to taste the sauce and tell me what it needs." He took my coat, like a real gentleman, and hung it in the closet. I followed him back to the kitchen.

He dipped sauce out of a pot bubbling on the

stove and held it out for me to taste. "Well?"

"Onion," I said. "Definitely needs onion. And thyme."

Dad sautéed some onion and scraped it into the pot. Then he snipped a few thyme leaves and added them, too. The room was quiet except for the blup-blup-blup of the sauce. Dad stirred and stirred.

"You should be on TV," I told him. "You could have your own show and call it . . . let's see . . . 'Terry's Terrific Tasting Tidbits.' "

He looked at me—one eyebrow up and one eyebrow down. It was a cool trick. The only other person I knew who could do it was Clark Gable, an old-time movie actor. "What are you talking about?" he said.

"Julia Child probably hauls in piles of money. She's famous. Wouldn't you like to be famous?"

"Naw. I love my humdrum life. Besides, if I were a TV celebrity I'd have to worry more about losing my hair. Bald heads don't look good on TV."

"Dad," I said after a bit.

"Hmmm?"

"I have a question."

He tasted a tablespoon of sauce. His eyes closed and his face relaxed. "Mmm! Exquisite—I've outdone myself." He flipped the burner heat down and looked at me. "Shoot."

"Did you ever . . . like someone you didn't know very well?"

Dad thought. "Yeah. Once. Years ago."

"What happened?"

"Not much. I was a mere youth at the time. Suddenly, there she was, the Woman of My Dreams. Eyes like green rhinestones, hair like black velvet. She was a beauty, all right."

"Did you talk to her?"

"You're not supposed to talk to girls you like from afar. You're just supposed to stand back and admire their wonderful qualities. I'm positive that's a rule of life that's written down somewhere. But, yes, I did talk to her."

This was interesting. I scooted to the edge of my chair, leaned my chin on my hands, and asked, "Well? What happened?"

Dad blushed. "She was the clerk at Dayton's fragrance counter—seventeen, sixteen at least. I was in junior high. For weeks I'd been hanging around, getting up the nerve to talk to her. One afternoon, when I was sure no one else was around, I went up to the glass counter and said—in the deepest voice I could muster—'Excuse me, miss. I'd like to sample the lime aftershave, please.' "

"What did she say?"

Dad stirred the sauce furiously and didn't look me in the eye. "She threw back her head and laughed this awful laugh—like a Chevy jammed in high gear. Finally she got her breath back. 'You?' she gasped. 'You? Hey, Harry, this little kid thinks he needs *shaving* lotion!' "

He sighed. "I don't blame her. I was just a skinny

thirteen year old, then. But it hurt. After that I was wiser about my infatuations." He sighed again. Then something occurred to him, and he gave me one of his sharp dad-looks. "Why do you ask?"

Luckily, Mom came into the kitchen right then. I swiveled in my chair and said, "Mom, how about you? Did you ever like a guy you hardly knew at all?"

"Sure. His name was Fred."

Parents have all these great secrets. All you have to do is ask the right questions.

"Fred?" my father asked. "You had a crush on someone named Fred?"

Mom smiled. "Yes. Fred Astaire. Talk about dreamy and romantic." She put her arms out and swooped around the kitchen like Ginger Rogers on a caffeine buzz. She stopped. "I used to watch his old films on the late show, and I thought he was gorgeous."

Kristie had used the same word to describe Max.

Dad was smirking, but I knew exactly what Mom was talking about. I have watched old Fred's movies on TV, too, and he is so debonair, charm oozes from every pore. That's something you can't say about many guys, especially the guys who go to Keats Junior High.

"But he was too old for you," I said. "Even back then he was too old for you."

"When you're in love—or like—you don't always consider little technicalities like that. And frankly,

Fred's maturity was his most appealing point. When I was in eighth grade, every boy in the vicinity was a hopeless dope."

I giggled. It killed me when my mom used words like dope.

Dad shouted up the stairs for Matthew to come for dinner, and in a few seconds we heard his clodhoppy feet on the steps. You don't have to call my brother for dinner twice.

"Why the sudden interest in our previous love lives, Vickie?" Mom said. She pretended to put finishing creases into the napkins at the table settings, but I knew she was sneaking looks at me.

"No big deal," I said, playing it casual. "Actually, there's this TV star named Max Adamms, and—"

"Max Adamms," Mom echoed. "Isn't he that adorable boy on 'For Goodness' Sake'?"

"Yup." Matthew suddenly bopped into the kitchen. "I watch that show every week. It's cool."

"He's pretty cute," I mumbled.

Dad carried the pot of spaghetti to the sink and dumped the contents into a collander. Steam rose around his head. "So you're smitten with Mr. Wonderful."

I went to my place and sat down. Mom and Matthew sat down, too.

"You have a crush on a TV star?" Mom asked.

I hated the sound of "crush." It seemed babyish, like "puppy love."

"I don't have a crush," I said. "Give me a break."

26

Dad appeared with a bowl of still-steaming spaghetti in his hands. "Forgive us for making that assumption. It's just that you get pink whenever his name is mentioned."

"You do!" Matthew yelped, peering into my face. "Vickie has a crush!"

How embarrassing. I blush way too much—a tendency I inherited from my dad. I didn't know why I was turning red, anyway, because I wasn't even sure if I liked Max yet. But I knew my family wouldn't let the conversation drop, so I said, "It's really Kristie, Janell, Chels, and Peg who are whipped on him. But I guess I don't blame them. The guy's middle name is cute."

They didn't scream or laugh or make funny faces, so I went on. "I read about him in Janell's fan magazine. He loves animals and always gets along with his parents and is naturally happy-go-lucky."

"No one is that perfect," Mom said. "No one even comes close. Not even Fred Astaire."

Dad flapped open his napkin. "I don't know," he said. "Sometimes I come close, don't I? Huh, Bobbie?"

"Well, Kristie thinks he's just about the greatest guy to hit planet Earth," I said. "She's really over the deep end."

Matthew suddenly blurted out, "I have a crush, too."

We all stared at him.

"Another girlfriend?" Dad asked. "Who is it this

time? Molly? Heather? Monique?"

"No," he said, dead serious. "Eleanor Roosevelt."

We all froze. No one dared look at anyone else for fear we'd burst out laughing. You have to be careful with little kids—they have these delicate feelings.

"Well," Dad said finally. "Mrs. Roosevelt was a remarkable woman. No wonder you admire her." He couldn't keep the corners of his lips from curling up, but at least he didn't laugh.

My brother started rattling on and on about Eleanor Roosevelt, and Mom and Dad smiled and said, "Uh huh," and "Really?" like it was the most fascinating stuff they had ever heard.

I just folded my hands and waited for Matthew to calm down so I could say grace. Imagine a kid having a crush on a dead person.

Eleanor Roosevelt. Unbelievable.

4

Later that night, Mom and I worked side by side stripping the poor old Christmas tree. I picked off the ornaments, and Mom put them in their boxes. We were a good team.

My cat, on the other hand, was lousy help. Bull-rush just sat on the couch watching us with his lazy eyes. Every once in a while his ear flicked. He didn't appreciate all the noise my brother and dad were making as they scooped the latest blizzard out of the driveway. Their shovels made flat "scraapes!" on the cement.

Mom held up a ratty-looking angel made from pipe cleaners. It had a bum leg where all the little hairs had been rubbed off, and its felt dress was dingy gray instead of white. "I remember when you made this. You were in kindergarten."

"It's a dog, Mom. We should throw it."

"Are you kidding? I wouldn't throw out this angel for all the popcorn in Iowa."

I said, "Oh, Mom," and pulled another bulb loose. Secretly I was relieved that she didn't want to junk it. It was comforting to see the same old decorations on the tree year after year, even if they were scruffy.

"This really makes me blue," she said, putting the angel lovingly into a box. "I hate putting away Christmas decorations."

"You think *you're* depressed," I said, reaching for a bulb hidden in the branches. "In a few short hours I'll open my eyes and there I'll be, right in the middle of science class, just as if I'd never left. Talk about depressing."

All during Christmas vacation I had kept school out of my mind, but tonight there was no escaping the truth. In a matter of hours, I'd be staring into a Petri dish full of fungus—all gray-fuzz-and-oozy-green. Gross.

"Relax," said Mom. "It's only Monday. School doesn't start until Wednesday."

"Relax? That's easy for you to say. You don't have to go back to homeroom and gym class and a locker so disorganized you can't even find your books."

I leaned over the couch and moaned, "Woe is me!" as if I were dying of anguish. I even pounded the couch cushions for dramatic effect.

I straightened up. Mom had gotten awfully quiet. My conscience gave me a good jab. As usual, I had jumped into my problems without asking about hers. Mothers are human, too.

"Tell me why you're depressed," I said. My sleeve was spiney with dry pine needles. I picked them off and waited patiently for her to speak.

She answered slowly, as if she were just now figuring it out. "It's not the decorations. They don't mean anything, not really. I just hate to see the season end. Folks seem happier at Christmastime."

It was true. In December, complete strangers smiled like they'd just been given a million dollars. At bus stops they stepped back to let each other board, and they cheerfully called "Merry Christmas" to people who got off.

After Christmas, things changed. People went back to their old ways. As a matter of fact, *I* went back to my old ways. It occurred to me that I had been in a crabby, post-Christmas mood for days.

Mom shook her head. "I'm absolutely positive that the joy of Christ's birth shouldn't end December 31st."

"But you don't expect people to be happy all of the time, do you, Mom? Because bad stuff happens. You can't expect folks to be jolly through . . . tornadoes, for instance. Or terrible diseases." I hopped around, flapping my arms. "Whee! Look at me! I've got leprosy!"

Mom giggled. "You've got the wrong idea, Miss Sarcastic. Joy isn't happiness. It's different. Joy doesn't depend on outside circumstances. It's . . . ongoing. A peacefulness in your heart."

Peacefulness in your heart. I liked that. I mulled the phrase around in my mind like a lemon drop on my tongue.

"Mom, if I told my friends that they should be joyful even when their homework isn't done and they've just flunked the big math test, they'd say I was whacko."

She laughed. "You're right. It only makes sense if you have faith in the Lord. Only He can give that kind of joy."

Come to think of it, Mom and Dad were joyful people. They had been sad when Jessica, my little sister, died before she was even born; things had been gloomy around our house for a long while. But even during the worst times, there had been peace in their hearts. They always believed that God would pull them through.

"Vickie," Mom said, "why the sudden glum face?"

"Now *I'm* depressed."

She laughed. "Why?"

"I wish I could be joyful."

"Maybe you'll have to work at it. Read about it. Pray about it. I'm sure that if you really want joy, you can have it."

"Really?" I wasn't convinced.

"Really."

Life was a mystery, all right, and probably the only human who had any answers was Dr. Angela Airhart. Mom and I worked silently awhile longer.

"Mom?"

"Huh?"

"You're right. People *don't* have the joy of Christmas all year, but at least there's a bright side."

"What bright side is that, O brilliant daughter?"

"At least we don't have to listen to 'Deck the Halls' over the mall speakers year round. Carols just wouldn't sound right in July."

"Ha! Ha! Ha!" Mom shouted, making Bullrush practically jump out of his skin. He bolted out of the room.

While I stared, Mom grabbed three silver bulbs out of the box and started juggling. She was an excellent juggler. For a woman with two kids—one of them being thirteen years old—Mom is a remarkably spunky woman. Her crinkled smile lines give her character.

The door opened and my dad and little brother came inside, knocking snow off their shoulders and stomping it from their boots.

"It's cold out there," Matthew informed us.

Mom shined a bulb. "I suppose we should feel guilty for sending them outside, Vickie."

"I don't feel a bit guilty," I said. "They drew the short straws, fair and square."

Dad pulled off his cap. His cheeks were red.

"Your compassion is overwhelming. What happened to your Christmas spirit?"

"As a matter of fact, we were just discussing that," Mom said.

"Uh-oh." Dad unzipped his coat. "A philosophical discussion. Count me out. My brain is frozen. It's in no condition for heavy thinking."

"But it's in great shape for marzipan," Matthew said, jumping up and down. He meant the highly sweet German candy that Dad makes only at Christmastime. Fancy chefs know how to do that sort of thing. "Right, Dad?" His wet hair bounced on his head. "Marzipan and milk!" Even I will admit my brother is occasionally cute and lovable, like other kids.

"Bring on the marzipan!" Dad shouted. "And make that cocoa instead of milk! Anyone else for a snack?"

"Oh," Mom groaned. "Sugar overload." But she raised her hand along with the rest of us.

Dad and Matthew went into the kitchen. We could hear them talking softly and banging cupboards. Bullrush came back and jumped onto the couch. The house was full of pleasant sounds and smells—milk, chocolate, pine—things people usually take for granted.

I smiled at Mom. Mom smiled at me. We kept working.

5

"I've been thinking," Chelsie said.

Janell, Kristie, Chels, Peggy, and I were sitting scrunched together on a mall bench. We all had slushes from the Whizzo ice cream counter, and from here we had a good view of the Big & Tall men's shop. We were hoping someone from school would walk by. Preferably a guy.

"Thinking?" asked Janell. "Amazing. What about?"

Chelsie chewed on her straw. She swallowed a few gulps of her slush. "I've been coming to this mall since I was a little kid. And it just now occurred to me that the Grandview Mall is anything *but*. Grand, I mean. It's kind of . . . mangey."

We looked around. The linoleum was clean but scuffed. The store signs were ancient.

"Yeah," said Kristie. "It never occurred to me either, but this place *is* pretty cruddy. But you can't name a mall Cheap and Junky Shopping Center. No one would be caught dead shopping in a place like that."

"How about Garbage Dump Square?" suggested Janell.

"Or Rat-Bait Plaza," I added.

We laughed—Chelsie her loud laugh, Peg her silly giggle, Janell and Kristie their similar, high-pitched wheezes. I laughed what Dad calls my belly laugh. Finally we quieted down again. From the bowling alley at the other end of the mall we heard the "Rollllll, Clunkkkkk!" of a bowling ball striking pins.

"But it's kind of a nice place anyway," I said. "Comfortable. Familiar. Like old socks. Or a good book. Maybe it all depends on how you look at it."

"Yeah," Kristie and Janell said together, nodding.

"Positive attitude," Chels said.

"Oh, look." Peg jumped up. "Is that Roy Goodrich? He's so cute. Tell me it isn't Roy Goodrich headed this way."

We all looked.

"It *isn't* Roy Goodrich," Janell said. "Get a hold of yourself, Peg."

"Oh." Peg sat down, disappointed. "I really thought it was him."

"This is so borrring," said Chelsie after another long silence. "Maybe we should go bowling or something."

Kristie moaned. "You wouldn't want to bowl if you were the bowling klutz of the universe, like me. Last time I went, I scored a total of 25 points."

"We wouldn't laugh at you," I told her. "Even if you only got *ten* points."

Kristie shook her head. "Sorry. My ego is too delicate. I can't take it."

"Scratch bowling," Chelsie said, sighing.

"We could go get a Coke," Kris suggested. "Over at the dime store counter."

"I'm swimming in liquid already," Janell said. "I feel like I'm on an inner tube on the Yangtze. One more thing to drink, and I'll float away." Janell likes to wow us with her knowledge of geography. She's big on major rivers and capital cities.

Peg stood up. She was on the lookout again.

"Well, at least I got some more magazines," said Kris, putting her hand inside the paper sack she held on her lap. She pulled out the new *Teen Fan* and some other magazine that had a big picture of Max Adamms splashed across the front. She flipped it open and started reading, slurping her slush. In a moment, she was gone to dream land.

The rest of us sat and stared at the shoppers. Little kids. Moms and dads. Babies in strollers. Elderly women with plastic shopping bags over their arms. Probably we were the only bored shoppers in the

37

whole place. Hanging out at the mall wasn't as much fun as it was supposed to be.

Suddenly Peg let out a yip. "Who's that?"

We looked. Instantly, Janell and Kristie—who were sitting on either side of me—gave me elbow jabs in the ribs.

It was Peter, the guy who had taught me all about kick-gliding in cross-country skiing, heading this way. Inside, I felt myself sinking into quicksand.

"Isn't that your friend?" Kristie asked. "Or should we say, your *boy*friend?"

As he moved closer, everyone sat very still, smiling into their slushes.

Peter looked right at me. "Hi, V—," he started to say. Then he realized that everyone was staring at him. He dropped his hand and ducked quickly into the Big & Tall shop. I was sure that Peter didn't wear big and tall clothes, but that's where he went.

As soon as he was out of sight, my friends exploded.

"Why are you blushing, Vic?" Janell asked. "Is Peter your boyfriend?"

The more I denied the stuff about boyfriends, the louder the teasing got. People passing stared. An elderly man went by and winked at me. I was about the size and color of a red ant. *Of all the people in the world to walk by,* I moaned to myself, *it had to be Peter.*

Everyone wanted to wait until he came out of the

store again, but he must have been trying on a pile of clothes. We waited for fifteen minutes and he never showed. Finally Chels jumped up.

"Come on, I'm bored spitless," she said. "Let's go. We can hit Peggy's house and watch New Year's Day parades. Preferably the ones in warm climates, like California."

We practically had to drag Kris by her hair. She was still reading up on all the new stuff about Max. Out on the street, she tried to turn pages with her mittened hands. "Listen to this," she said. "There's a book coming out—all about him. It's a kind of picture scrapbook. And he's going on a tour to promote it. It says here he'll be at the Great Books bookstore in St. Paul on January 13."

We all stopped and stared at each other like zombies.

"That's . . ." The wind whipped Chelsie's hair around. "That's only two weeks away!"

Kristie's mouth dropped open. Her tongue was stained purple from the slush. "That means we'll see him. In the flesh."

We all let out a scream at the same time.

Then we stood around and absorbed this new information silently. We must have looked pretty strange standing there in the parking lot like a herd of sheep.

"Great Books bookstore is out in the boonies," I said.

"Who cares?" Kris roared at me. "I'd follow him

to the ends of the earth." She stopped. "This means that as the president of his local fan club, I'll get to meet him. I'll get to shake his hand."

My palm got sweaty just thinking about it. Thank goodness *I* wasn't the fan club president. Maybe I could just wave at him from a distance.

We turned around and went back inside to the bookstore to see if we could find the book. Kristie bought a copy. She felt responsible, she said, on account of her being the president and all. I couldn't have bought it, as I am always low on funds. Besides, Kris promised we could each borrow it overnight. We sat on a bench and went through it page by page.

Then it was time to head for Peg's. As we trudged along the sidewalk, Kristie floated behind us. I don't think her boots touched snow all the way there.

6

"Bzzzzzzzzzzzz!!!"

My alarm clock screamed its head off, and I pulled my hand out from under my pillow and slapped the clock silly.

Then I moaned and rolled over, trying to blink my brain into action. Ah. Wednesday morning; my first day back at school. Outside it was dark. The wind rattled the window. I felt totally miserable. But I sat up and swung my warm feet into the cold, cruel world.

I was rummaging in my dark closet for something to wear when the idea hit me, just came into my head. A way to survive my first day back at school: I would put myself in an all-day mellow mood. I had heard of people doing that. Today I'd be so relaxed, nothing would bother me—not even gymnastics. With any luck I wouldn't even realize I had been in school until the day was over.

I dressed and ate, then waited for Chelsie at the front door, trying to get into the right mood. First, I needed to think of something peaceful. Hmmm. I closed my eyes. As soon as I did that my head started swimming back to sleep. I opened my eyes again, and put my brain into high thinking gear (which I hadn't done since vacation started). Finally I had the answer. I would pretend I was surrounded by a soap bubble. That way I'd be protected from everything. Yeah, that might work.

"Hey, Vic! Come on!"

It was Chelsie, waving from the front gate. I stepped outside. It was fierce January. Balloon-like, I floated down the sidewalk in my coat and mittens.

"Hiya-hiya," she shouted.

"Hello," I said.

We crunched along.

"What's with you?" she asked.

"Nothing. I'm great. I'm fine."

We kept walking. "Something's wrong with you." She peered into my face. "Are you sick?"

"Nope."

"Well, how come you're acting like a goon?" Whenever Chelsie gets bugged her left nostril twitches. Just now her nostril was twitching like crazy. "You're totally spacey!"

"I don't know what you mean." I kept my voice breathy so it wouldn't disturb my feeling of soap-bubble calmness.

"Victoria Hope Mahoney. I'm your best friend. Right? When I say you're being weird, I know what I'm talking about. Right? Right. And I say you're acting like some airhead."

"Thanks a lot!" I said in my real voice.

"That's better." She sounded relieved.

"Chelsie," I said, hugging my books, though what I really wanted to do was throw them into a snowdrift. "I was *trying* to get myself into a good mood for school. I was imagining that I was in a big soap bubble."

"Well, don't do it again. It was scary. Anyway, I don't think you can fake a good mood."

A bus roared by, blasting fumes in our direction. "Some people do it," I said, thinking of Mattie Baker. "Some people are always in a good mood."

"That's true," Chelsie said. "But I betcha they mean it. I bet it's real and not fake." We were quiet, thinking it over.

"I'm talking about more than good moods," I told her, struggling to make myself clear. "I mean joy. Mom and I were having this conversation about joy, and—"

"Joy who?"

"Not who. What."

"Oh. I thought you were talking about that conceited girl who works in the cafeteria."

"No. Pay attention."

"Okay, Vic. Shoot."

"It's a . . . a peacefulness in your heart. That's how Mom put it."

She shook her head. "I don't think I've got that—I can be a real crab sometimes."

I said, "You can say that again," and then ducked when she tried to punch me.

We fought the wind awhile before talking again. The streetlight up ahead turned green, signaling us across the street.

"I'd like to be joyful all the time," I declared. "Even when it's not Christmastime. Even when things aren't jolly."

Chels whistled. "That's a tall order, kid. You're only human."

In the dark, Keats Junior High School was bursting with light. Every window was yellow. Chelsie held the door open for me, and I went into the heavy warm air, stomping snow off my boots.

There were kids rushing everywhere. They weaved in and out, zigzagged, cut left, slid to sudden stops. The air was thick with laughter. Chels and I walked straight toward our lockers. The halls felt smaller than I remembered. Cramped, like a too-tight Band-Aid.

"Back to the real world, eh, Vic?" Chelsie said to me.

I nodded, my joyful intentions shriveling into nothing in an instant.

44

The smell of new clothes was in the air. I was wearing cool new boots, but so far no one had noticed. Everyone was too busy worrying about who was noticing *their* clothes.

A pinching hand grabbed my elbow. It was Kristie, who had sneaked up behind us.

"You have to see this!" she said, dragging us along. She fiddled with her locker combination and swung open the door.

"Voilà!" she shouted.

"Wow," said Chelsie. "It's great."

"It's Max," I said.

She had covered the whole inside of her locker door with posters.

"And listen to this," she told us. "I'm working on the first official fan club newsletter. Be waiting by those mailboxes. Gotta run. See you at lunch."

Someone walked by with a radio turned *way* up. Radios are not allowed in Keats, but I hear music a lot. I wondered if anyone ever listened to Dr. Angie. Probably not. Chels hummed along with the song as she worked on her locker combination. For a moment I couldn't remember my number, but it came back to me. Chels kept humming. She stacked her books on the top shelf and gave each one a cheerful shove inside. They went "Bang!" as they hit the back of the locker. Every once in awhile she turned and shouted, "Howdy!" to a friend passing.

"You're in a chipper mood," I said.

"I'm pretending I'm in a giant soap bubble," she

said, flapping her arms gracefully. "Ooo, look at me. I'm flying."

"Cut it out."

Chelsie slammed her door. "I've got to scram. See ya, Vic, old buddy. Be joyful!" She took off.

Standing there alone, I felt a tiny pang of loneliness. Then a microscopic stab of excitement. Followed by a great wave of curiosity. What would happen today? I was a confused mess, all right. Angie would have her work cut out for her, straightening me out. Digging a few crumpled papers out of the bottom of my locker, I prayed silently. "Well, God," I said. "Here I go. Hang around, would You?"

First period nearly put me back to sleep. The teacher looked exhausted, as if he personally had rung in the new year. But soon enough the bell was ringing, setting us free again.

I made a quick stop in the science room to check on my fungus, which had definitely made progress over vacation. Gross. I almost threw up.

In the hall, I ran into an old friend. Peter. Of the humiliating mall experience.

We were both zoning in on the same drinking fountain, and by the time we saw each other it was too late to turn around. He got there first. I waited. He kept drinking and drinking. I think he was stalling for time. Finally he stood up, water dripping frm his chin.

"Hi," he said.

At first he wouldn't look right at me. I didn't take offense. Sometimes I'm shy when I first see someone after a long time.

"That was you at the mall, wasn't it?" I asked. Very casual.

"Yeah," he said with a scowl, as if he were answering a very tough math question. "That was me. Was that you?"

Boy. This was one terrific conversation. "Yep," I said. "Yours truly."

The one thing I couldn't do was ask old Peter why he had ignored me at the mall. That would have been uncouth. Dumb, too, because actually I understood, in a way. By himself, Peter was a pal. We weren't best friends, like Chels and me, but we sometimes hung around and stuff. As soon as our friends appeared, it was important to act casual. I didn't blame him for not waving or stopping to talk at the mall.

"You have a good Christmas?" he asked.

"Yeah," I said. "Pretty good."

"My dad and I caroled our whole neighborhood. We took Snoozer, my dog. Remember him? While Dad and I sang, Snooze howled. He drowned us out."

I could just picture it. For a second or two I laughed like a hyena. Peter did, too. His face kind of loosened up.

"I got skis," I said. "Not expensive, but they work."

47

"Hey, maybe on Saturday we could ski down by the lake. There's a warming house down there for the skaters. We could go in and thaw out if we got frozen."

"Yeah, great," I said, relieved that we were talking like old friends. Like buddies. This boy-girl stuff was exhausting.

"Meet me at the warming house at ten-thirty, Saturday morning. Okay?"

"Yeah, okay."

A bunch of kids were coming, slamming lockers and shouting. "Maybe I'll see you around," I said to Peter.

"Yeah," he said, relief crossing his face like a shadow. "Maybe." He took off.

I shot down the hall. Only six more periods to go.

7

After school I took the bus to my grandma's apartment, just for the fun of it. I have to keep track of Isadora and her new husband Harold. If I don't, I miss important stuff.

The elevator shot me straight up to the twenty-fifth floor. The doors closed behind me, and I was alone in a quiet hall. I edged over to the window to take a peek. Heights make me dizzy, but in a swing-ing-too-high, thrill-in-the-pit-of-the-stomach sort of way.

The hallway to the apartment was dingy-dark. I walked slowly past the doorways. Behind 2500, a woman's voice sang "Ramona," a song my dad taught me when I was little. The song faded as I hurried past. A bird squawked in apartment 2511. Someday I hoped to get a peek at that bird, maybe teach it to say my name. In 2515 silverware clanked as it was put into drawers or set around a table. And as I passed 2520, a boy wearing a black paper stovepipe hat and a glued-on beard charged out of the door, almost knocking me down. At the last second I ducked to one side and he headed for the elevator reciting, "Fourscore and seven years ago—" Sometimes I wouldn't mind living in an apartment building. There's lots going on.

At 2525, I knocked. Waited. No one came to the door. I fished out my key and jammed it into the lock. The door eased open.

Sometimes, when no one was home, I pretended it was my place. I would make myself a cup of Red Zinger tea and choose a TV show. What luxury. Without my brother whining to change the channel, I felt completely free.

I latched the door behind me and looked around. A lot of grandmothers I know have doilies and crocheted blankets around. Not Isadora. The joint was crammed with funky furniture and decorated with her paintings.

Back in November, when Isadora married my old friend Harold Wilkes (who was as peculiar as Isadora, in a lovable sort of way), they pooled their belongings. They came up with a wild collection of stuff. Vases full of dried pussy willows, piles of paperbacks, five antique telephones, wooden animal carvings from Mexico, brass bells from India, ugly plants with hairy leaves, and one giant loom which stood silently in a corner of the living room. Clutter didn't bother Isadora and Harold. I dumped my books onto the kitchen table.

"Hi, small fry," a muffled voice said.

I jumped into the sky with a shriek.

Isadora emerged, back end first, from a cupboard. She was grinning. "Scare you?"

"Only to death," I said. "But don't worry about me. I didn't suffer long."

She pushed her springy gray hair back inside her scarf and stood there with her hands on her hips. "I didn't hear you knock. I was rooting around for these old cookbooks. Sit down, I want to talk to you about something."

"But—"

She dropped a pile of the books onto the table. "I'm planning a party."

"What for? I'm still worn out from your wedding reception."

She smiled fondly. "That *was* fun, wasn't it? We partied hard, that's for sure. But this is different. This party is for old friends. People who graduated from college with Harold and me."

I did some arithmetic. Isadora and Harold would have been college students in the forties. Wow. I almost asked, "They're still *alive?*" but I caught myself in time. *Of course they're alive, Victoria, you idiot. Isadora and Harold are. And they don't seem*

51

old, not really. Not for grandparent-types.

"Hey, that could be a riot," I said. "Do you know where everyone is?"

"Mostly. I'm going to call my old pals, and Harold will call his. Most of them live here in town. It's going to be a costume party. They have to wear the clothes they wore in college—or reasonable facsimiles. Isn't that a scream?" She slapped the table and hee-hawed.

"Here's where you come in, Victoria. Will you help serve food that night? Harold and I will be busy hobnobbing."

"Sure," I said. "Can I wear a costume? I could dress like a maid."

"Of course! Of course! I'll dredge up a uniform for you. I've got boxes full of stuff."

That didn't surprise me.

"Stay for dinner, Victoria. Harold is teaching a craft class at the senior citizens' center tonight, and you and I have a lot of planning to do."

I dialed Mom up fast. She didn't care, she said, because she had only spent hours putting together the dinner of my dreams. Very sarcastic.

"I'm just kidding," she added. "Wait a minute, Matthew wants to talk."

"Hi, Vickie?" said my brother's voice. "Where are you?"

"I'm at Isadora's," I told him, "and no, you can't come over. Iz and I are planning an important event. No kids allowed."

"I don't care," he said. "Because Mom and I are having crab sandwiches. With sprouts. Nyah, nyah. Put Isadora on the phone. I want to talk to her."

I handed the receiver over. When she heard my brother's voice, Isadora's face went all soft and smiley like a grandma's. She even called him "sweetheart," which he definitely is not.

"Really?" she was saying. "I had no idea Eleanor Roosevelt did all *that*."

I rolled my eyes and started clearing the table of cookbooks. He was at it again.

Together my grandma and I cooked up a batch of soup. Into the boiling pot of water and chicken stock we dropped onions, potatoes, parsley, carrots, and chicken. Isadora handled the spices. I don't know what all she added, but it smelled wonderful. Finally we sat down at the little table with steaming hot bowls at our places, plus thick hunks of bread on plates.

During dinner I told Iz all about Max Adamms. She had never heard of him, so I filled her in on all the details. She nodded and nodded.

As I talked, a little twang of excitement kept jabbing me in the gut, and my mouth smirked uncontrollably. Was I falling-in-like with Max for real, just like Janell, Peg, Kris, and Chels? Up until now I'd sort of been playing along. It would be a relief if I could feel about him the way all my friends did.

Just as long as I didn't get as bad as Kristie, that is. That would be too much!

53

8

Saturday was a frosty one, but the sun was shining like mad. I smiled as I checked out the weather from my bedroom window. "Thank You, Lord."

Peter was already waiting by the warming house when I waved at him from the top of the slope.

"You're late," he yelled up at me.

"It's only 10:31!" I shouted back.

"Hurry up!"

Together, we hit the tracks. We sped along. We glided. We dipped down hills and then shot up to the top. I couldn't believe it was already noon when old Peter said, "Let's take a break. I'm starved."

The warm-up house wasn't crowded—just a couple of little kids lacing up their ice skates. While

Peter unpacked a backpack full of food, I helped them get the laces tight. I am an old lace-up pro.

"Here you go," Pete said, handing me a plastic bag. It was full of cracker sandwiches: banana slices and peanut butter. The Thermos kept a batch of tomato soup hot. And the best part was for dessert: a whole chocolate bar for each of us. Everything was delicious, and I'm not easily impressed. When your father is a chef, you can get pretty picky about food.

I swallowed some soup. "It's superb," I told him, blinking as the steam rose from the Thermos cup into my eyes. "You put together a mean lunch."

"Yep, packed it myself," he said. His words were jumbled on account of a big mouthful of peanut butter.

Afterward, we hit the slopes again and skiied until we were whipped. I was glad to get home all right. My cheeks needed to unthaw.

"So long," I yelled from the front gate. I hoped my parents weren't at the living room window, cooing parental stuff like, "Aren't they cute?" But even if they were, I didn't care. Having old Pete as a friend was just fun.

Besides the fact that I was frozen, I had another reason for rushing home. I had a new Max picture to hang up. Kris had dropped it off that morning.

I dashed for my room. The poster was still there, folded up in a neat square on my desk. Very carefully I unfolded it. Max Adamms, in person. In this picture, he was looking sideways at the camera, holding a cowboy hat on his head. It must have been a windy day in Hollywood or something.

I knew just the perfect spot for it—on the wall above my desk. That way I could look up whenever I needed a break from my homework. I pushed a tack into each corner. Then I stood back. Gorgeous.

"Who's that?" Matthew bopped into my bedroom. He has this tendency to appear out of nowhere—like the flu.

"You know who it is, Matthew. It's Max Adamms."

"Oh, yeah," he said, squinting at Max. "I didn't recognize him in that hat." Then he dove onto my bed, slapped his hands behind his head, and heaved a big sigh. Obviously he planned on spending some time.

"Vickie?" he asked.

"Yeah?"

"Is Max Adamms your boyfriend?"

Having a brother like Matthew is very strange. I used to think he was a giant pest. But now that he is getting older, he is also getting smarter. Every once in awhile he asks a question that cuts me right back to a nub. In situations like this, calmness is the trick. I sat down at my desk and shuffled some homework around. "No, not really."

"Well . . . are you in love with him?"

Was I? I had all the symptoms. I thought about him during class. I read every word in the fan magazines that I could get my hands on. And now I had his picture up on my wall. Still, it didn't feel like true love.

I stared Max right in the eye. He peered back, not moving a muscle. Sometimes this felt like a very one-sided relationship.

"To tell the truth, Matthew, I don't know if I'm in love with him or not."

My brother nodded as if he knew exactly what I meant. "Hey," he said. "Where'd you get the poster, anyway?"

"From Kristie. She has a whole stash." Kris hadn't wanted to part with her posters, but the members of the Max Adamms Fan Club had put pressure on her. Look, we said, not everyone can afford magazines. At least you could share with the less fortunate. That got to her. She forked over one tear-out magazine poster for each of us.

"Do you think she could get me a poster of Mrs. Roosevelt?" Matthew asked. "Just a little one. It doesn't even have to be in color."

I looked at my little brother. He was up on one elbow, giving me this bright-and-hopeful face. If he had been my kid, I probably would have hugged him or something.

As his older sister I tried to explain the concept of fan magazines to him—very slowly, so he'd get it. ("They have articles about stars, mostly *guy* stars, who are still *alive*.") But he just looked at me, his mouth hanging open. It was an "I-don't-get-it" expression if I ever saw one.

"I'll try to find a picture," I finally promised. Anything to make him stop looking so pathetic. Then I added, "Listen, Matthew. What's so great about Eleanor Roosevelt, anyway?"

He told me what a smart lady she had been. She had tramped all over the country, rooting for the poor. You had to hand it to her. She'd thrown her heart and soul into her work. When Matthew finished his speech I thought, for one crazy moment, that *I* wouldn't mind a poster of Eleanor Roosevelt.

Matthew scrambled off the bed. "I know you'd like me to stay," he said, "but I've got just tons of things to do." And he was gone.

Ah, the room to myself. I jumped onto the warm spot on my bed. The buzz from the skiing was fading, and I felt sleepy and comfortable. It was stare-down time for old Max.

Just for fun, I played a little game. My imagination pasted a make-believe poster of Peter right up there alongside Max. Then I compared them.

Max was the tallest. At least that's what I assumed. Actually it was pretty hard to tell, because in the picture he wasn't standing next to anything. He just *looked* tall, somehow. The hair showing under his hat was longish and perfectly brushed.

Peter, on the other hand, was a little on the short side. (I decided not to hold that against him, since I am on the short side, too.) He didn't want to be a TV star. More likely he wanted to become a famous soccer player. His hair was black, just like Max's, but somehow it wasn't as perfect. It looked like maybe he had slept on it funny. Probably that was considered bad news on the cuteness scale. He didn't dress nearly as cool as Max; mostly he wore old jeans and big sweatshirts. There was no comparison.

I sighed. I absolutely didn't feel about Peter the way I did about Max. Maybe I really was in love with Max. Life was a mystery, all right. *Maybe*, I thought, *Maybe I will actually have to call Dr. Airhart.*

"So, Doc," I could hear myself saying. "I've got these, well, sort-of, feelings about a world-famous TV star, and I was just wondering if you could help me."

("Hmm," was all she would say, so I'd continue to spill my guts.)

"—Tell me, Doctor. Am I crazy or what? I've fallen for Mr. Perfect from TV-land, but I still like to have real, live normal guys like Peter around, too. Is that strange or what?"

That one would stump old Angie.

9

The note was shoved through the vent in my locker. "Fan Club meeting at lunch. Usual table. Be there." It was in President Kristie's writing.

I was the last one to arrive, and the club members were already heavily into a debate. Kris was shaking her fork at the others.

"What's up?" I asked, sliding in.

Janell turned to me. "Kris has this fantasy that we should drive out to California to meet Max."

Stunned, I looked around the table at faces to see if they were kidding. They looked serious.

"Just a short trip," Kris explained. "During the summer." She picked up speed as she talked, like she was afraid someone would stop her if she paused too long. "We wouldn't be gone long. We could hang around outside the studio where Max films the show. The rest of the day we could go to the beach. Wouldn't it be fun?"

"It'd be great," I said. "Except for one thing."

"What's that?"

"It's crazy!"

Chels nodded. "I hate to say it, but Vic is right. You think our parents are going to go for this scheme? Not in this lifetime. Parents don't appreciate their daughters traveling cross-country to drop in on movie stars."

"Besides," I pointed out, "they don't film sitcoms during the summer."

"Well . . ." Kristie switched strategies quickly. "We could find out what restaurants he eats at and hang out there." She was lost in thought. "Let's see. How many cars would we need?"

Peg tapped her fingernail on the formica table for attention. "If we rented a bus, it'd be cheaper than driving a bunch of cars."

"Yeah," Kristie added, "and we could pool baby-sitting money for gas, and—"

Suddenly Chelsie tossed a fork onto her plastic lunch tray. It made a loud, impatient clatter. We turned and looked at her.

"You're also forgetting one very important point. Who's going to drive this bus, for Pete's sake? We don't have licenses, in case you'd all forgotten."

We sat staring at our laps. But in a flash Kristie

61

had the answer. She whumped her hand down flat on the table. "We'll hire someone. Like a chauffeur. Janell's brother, for instance. He has a driver's license."

"Oh, no," Janell said, her mouth full of lunch. "I'm not traveling 2000 miles with my brother. We'd fight the whole way. I couldn't do it, not even for Max. No, sir."

"Better idea?" Chels asked.

"I've got it," Janell said. "We get some parents to chaperone us. Parents feel more secure if their kids are chaperoned."

"It's possible," said Peggy skeptically. "But who?"

All at once, they turned to me.

"What?" I asked.

"Of all the possible parents, yours are the most logical choice," said Chels. "They actually like kids. A busload of teenagers would be my parents' idea of a 'Twilight Zone' nightmare. Your parents, on the other hand, are a scream. They might do it."

"I don't think so."

"Just ask them," Chels said. "You're our only hope."

"For our sakes," said Janell. Her face was desperate.

"As your president," said Kristie, "I'm begging you."

"Oh, all right," Janell said suddenly, and everyone turned from me to her. "I'll ask my parents.

And if that doesn't work, I'll even"—she grimaced—"try my brother."

Peggy had a gigantic smile on her face. "You know, Janell, your brother is kind of cute."

"Peg, you think every guy is cute." Janell screwed up her face. "But my brother?" She pretended to jab her finger down her throat. "That's positively nauseating."

We picked up our forks to eat. We'd forgotten about food in the excitement over our California plans.

When I got home that night, some funny-looking clothes were spread out on the couch. The smell of mothballs was in the air. I closed the door and eavesdropped on the voices in the kitchen. Then I remembered that Harold and Isadora were invited to dinner.

Izzy rushed out to meet me.

"Look at this," she said, steering me over to the couch before I could make a move. "This is your maid costume for the party." It was black. There was also a little white apron. I yanked off my coat, grabbed the dress, and shut myself in the closet. It was stuffy in there, and hangers kept banging into my head. Finally I got the dress on.

"Ta-da!" I shouted, bursting out.

Isadora zipped me up and then surveyed me like I was one of her paintings. "Not too bad," she pronounced, after a long silence.

I shoved my feet into the high-heeled shoes. I

jumbled with the skinny ankle straps and finally got them latched. The shoes were gigantic. I clunked around the room in them. "May I offer you an hors d'oeurve, ma'am?" I asked Isadora, holding out an imaginary tray.

"Watch yourself," Grandpa Harold said, coming into the room. "Don't want to fracture an ankle in those stilts."

Isadora frowned. "Yes, they really are too big for her. I'll have to come up with something else. Otherwise you look authentic, Victoria."

"This will be hysterical," I said, undoing the shoes. "When's the party?"

"Saturday after next. Can you make it?"

"Sure."

Mom shouted out from the kitchen. "Vickie, your father's working tonight. Do you want to practice your waitressing abilities by helping me serve dinner?"

"One moment, madam," I said, charging back into the closet.

During dinner I was quiet, thinking of a way to bring up the California trip. It seemed sort of touchy, I don't know why. I guess I'm getting more experienced dealing with parents. I kept waiting for the right minute. Not yet, I told myself, heaping Brussels sprouts onto my plate. Sometimes when I'm nervous I eat like a fiend. And I don't even like Brussels sprouts. No one noticed, though. They were all ranting about the forties party. Isadora had

64

found a hair stylist who would comb her old wig into a forties hair style—with a snood and everything.

"A snood?" Matthew asked. "What's that?"

We all got into a laughing fit over the word snood, while poor Isadora tried to explain that it was a bag-like net that caught the ends of a woman's hair. We laughed right over her explanation.

I never did get up the courage to mention the trip. Maybe I'd just wait and see if everything would work out. That's something parents usually like to do.

Just wait and see.

10

"It's not fair," said Peggy, digging her hand into the popcorn bowl. "I had my heart set on going to California."

The theme song to "For Goodness' Sake" was blasting out of the TV, and she had to shout to be heard. Gloomily we sat and watched the credits roll by.

We were drowning our sorrows in television because Janell's parents had said no, they were *not* driving her to California, and what's more, no one else was either. A thirteen-year-old had no business traipsing across the country in a bus, and— There was more, but Janell said it was too depressing to repeat. I wasn't surprised at the news. It seemed like

Janell's parents had behaved normally, which was comforting in a strange sort of way.

During the commercial we sat and picked at the carpet in Chelsie's bedroom. Mr. Bixler had wheeled the TV in for us. "Have fun," he told us and left. I guess the Bixlers weren't into "For Goodness' Sake."

"Well," said Chelsie, "it was a sort of far-fetched idea."

"—And," Kristie added, "Max *is* going to be in town in less than a week. Let's see, today is Tuesday. Saturday is only three days away if you don't count the rest of today or the day Max gets in—"

"My dad offered to pick you all up Saturday morning and drive us to the mall," I said.

"Not the same as taking us to California," Janell pointed out.

"No," said Chels, "but still a nice gesture. Tell your father we appreciate it."

"Okay."

"Shh-shh-shh-!" Peg elbowed us. "It's starting!"

We glued our eyeballs to the set. You couldn't have pried us loose with a crowbar.

At the next commerical, Mrs. Bixler came in. She filled the doorway. She is a tall person. We all looked up at her.

"Hello, girls," she said.

I noticed that she had a whole tray of food.

"How about some more refreshments?" The only person I know who would use the word refresh-

67

ments is Mrs. Bixler. But I like her. She's an unusual person. She lowered the tray, and the whole thing was covered with hand-made appetizers. Wow. I grabbed the nearest one. It was a cracker layered with the thinnest slice of lox, which is smoked salmon. Plus there was some kind of sauce and the tiniest sprig of dill. Very elegant—and expensive, too. Leave it to Mrs. Bixler to serve us fancy snacks. Even Dad's eyes would have bugged out of his head if he saw this—and he fiddles with food all the time.

"How's the show?" she wanted to know.

"All right," we all mumbled, but we knew any program with Max in it was better than all right.

"If you don't mind, I think I'll just watch a little of this show with you. I've never actually seen this young man Chelsie has been talking about."

Mrs. Bixler took a seat on the bed. "Is there anything else I can get you?" she asked us. Boy. For a woman who supposedly didn't care for teenagers, she was doing really well.

After about a hundred commercials, the show started again.

"Is that the boy?" asked Mrs. Bixler. "The one with the dreamy eyes? Look how green his eyes are."

"I heard that he wears colored contacts," said Janell. "The producers of the show said he could switch colors as often as he wanted, as long as he stuck to just one color per episode."

"You don't say?" breathed Mrs. Bixler. She was

really interested. "That's Hollywood for you."

The story line was about a visiting cousin who turned out to be a thief. Of course Max solved the mystery and gave a speech about how it was wrong to steal. He put that cousin in his place, all right.

"Well," said Chelsie's mom, standing up and smoothing her sweater down. "That was certainly enjoyable. Chelsie was right. He is cute. I can definitely see the appeal of your young heartthrob. I'll leave you girls to it, now. Let me know if there's anything else you need."

When I got home there was a message for me on the kitchen counter. Peter had called. Probably he wanted to set up another ski outing. I had forgotten all about him, which just goes to show how fickle some people can be. It was sort of late, so I decided to wait until the next day to call. I mean, he was just a normal guy. He wasn't a movie star or anything.

11

Thunk. Thunk. Thunk. The whole house shook and rumbled under my feet each time I hit the floor. It was a very satisfying sound, I thought, as the jump rope sailed over my head. Between breaths, I counted my jumps aloud: ". . . forty, forty-one, forty-two . . ."

My bedroom door swung open, and Mom stood in the doorway. "What are you doing?" she demanded.

I kept jumping. "Jumping rope," I said, "Forty-four, forty-five . . ."

"I know you're jumping rope, Ms. Smarty. I came to find out *why* you're doing it at eight o'clock on a Wednesday night. Your father and I get precious little quiet around this house; why would you want to disturb our one real opportunity for relaxation?"

"Forty-eight, forty-nine, fif— Oh, rats!" The jump rope whapped my leg, I tripped, and the thunks stopped. Mom just stood there, her arms crossed. I faced her, gasping for breath.

"I am jumping rope because, well, for . . . a variety of reasons."

"Name one."

I paused. How was I going to phrase this without sounding like an idiot?

Mom, waiting for me to speak, made a suggestion. "Are you suddenly joining the ranks of the physically fit?"

"Sort of."

"Sort of?"

I said the next part fast. "Also I read that physical activity is good for depression."

She got a concerned look, just like the one mothers in aspirin commercials get when their kids have fevers. "It is. But, honey, why are you depressed?"

"I'm not actually depressed."

Mom put her hand over her face and shook her head. "You've lost me, Victoria. Start again and go slowly. What is this all about?"

"Just look at me."

She looked. "You seem okay to me. A little sweaty, but other than that, okay."

Gross. I could have lived without the sweaty

comment. "But I'm not exactly the picture of joy, am I?"

"Well, the left side of your lower lip *is* turning down instead of up."

"See? Ever since we talked about being joyful, I've been trying, Mom. I really have. But have you seen me hopping around and singing?"

"No."

"Have you seen me grinning from ear to ear?"

"Not much. You have a sort of small smile actually. It's more like your father's than mine."

"I rest my case," I said. "Some joyful person."

Mom leaned against the door, arms crossed, and her eyebrows scrunched together. She was thinking about something heavy. "But, Vickie, big grins and loud singing aren't the only ways people show joy. Sometimes joy is boisterous, of course. But other times it can be quiet. Heartfelt. I bet joy could even make you smile inside without the smile ever hitting your lips. Even through the bad times, a joyful Christian has hope."

Hmm, I thought. *Hope*. I was hopeful that I'd get to see Max Adamms on Saturday, and maybe get his autograph. Did that make me a joyful Christian? My brain felt milky and dull.

"Listen to this," I told her. "Just yesterday, my joy level dropped to an all-time low. And all because the stupid California trip was cancelled."

Mom straightened up, looking slightly stunned. "*What* California trip?"

I explained the whole thing. When I got to the part about Janell's brother at the wheel of a rented bus, she went a little white, but she didn't make a peep. Just nodded her head. The thing I appreciate about my mom is that she listens.

"And the crazy thing, Mom—"

"Hmm?"

"I wasn't even sure I wanted to go. It was sort of a wild plan."

"Sort of," she agreed. She plunked down on the edge of my bed. "But no one said you can't feel disappointed once in awhile. God will give you the strength to fight back. That way you don't ever completely lose hope. Does that make sense?"

Yeah, I thought, but it doesn't mean it will work for me.

Mom tapped her forehead. "Think about it."

Together, Mom and I prayed that I'd learn a thing or two about joy. I have always felt that talking to God is a very comforting pastime. ("Yes, yes," I imagined Him saying. "I see what you mean," or "Hmm. You don't say? Well, I know exactly what you're talking about.") In my family, we always pray as if God were right there in the room, or maybe on the telephone line.

Afterward Mom gave me a long hug and headed for the door. Then she had another thought. "And in the future, when you decide to become physically fit, do it in the basement, okay?"

12

Dahlia's Diner was packed to the gills. Chelsie and I wedged ourselves in the front door and peered around. The hostess, a woman with black eyeliner and matching black hair piled on top of her head, gave us the once-over.

"Table for five," Chels and I said together. "We're meeting some friends."

The woman squinted and radared the room with her sharp eyes. "Sorry," she said. "Don't have a table open at the moment. You'll have to wait."

We added our name to the list. Chelsie gave them Bixler because it seemed easier to spell than Mahoney.

"It's only six-fifteen," I said to Chelsie, checking

my watch. "We've got plenty of time before first period."

Chelsie stretched her neck over the crowd of waiting people. "I don't see the gang. They better show. If I dragged my carcass out of bed at five-thirty a.m. for no good reason, I will be furious."

The door opened, and the other three members of the Max Adamms fan club came stomping in.

"We're here!" Janell announced, holding her arms out as if she were going to give everyone in the restaurant a giant hug.

"Keep your voice down," Kris said, shrinking. "You're humiliating us."

"What?" Janell looked around innocently. "I'm just a warm and caring person—who happens to have a voice that carries."

"You're also a nut case," said Chelsie.

Just then, our hostess gave us the wave and we tromped behind her to an empty booth. Janell accidentally banged somebody's knees with her trombone case. The waiting lobby crowd glared at us.

"You realize why we were seated first, don't you?" asked Janell, whipping open her napkin and tucking it into her collar. "Because I made a scene. As my father always says, 'The squeaky wheel gets the grease.' You should thank me."

"Just behave now," Peg said, scooching in beside her. "Remember your manners. And take that stupid napkin off. You look silly." Peg is from the South, where, I hear, manners are very big. She even calls my parents "ma'am" and "sir."

"All right, all right," said Kris. "Enough chatter. I call this Max Adamms Fan Club Meeting to order."

"You're so professional," said Chels, clasping her hands together and fluttering her eyelashes at Kristie.

"Cut it out." Kris pushed her away, annoyed. "Be serious. Maybe I'm the only one who realizes that this is our last meeting before Max flies into town this Saturday." She put a lot of emphasis on the words "this Saturday," which made us all quiet.

The waitress came and we ordered five coffees, even though Chels and I are the only ones who actually like to drink the stuff.

"Now," continued Kristie, pushing her hair efficiently behind her ears. "Let's take care of business. Vickie, your father is going to pick us all up?"

"Right," I said. "First Chelsie, because she lives closest. Then everyone else."

"Okay. Can we count on you sometime between nine-forty-five and nine-fifty?"

"Correct, chief."

Kris made a check in her notebook. "Now. I'll bring my book for Max to autograph. The rest of you will have to use your posters. Is that clear?"

"Absolutely," said Chelsie.

"Yes, ma'am," Peg said.

"Clear," I answered, giving a salute.

"Like mud," said Janell.

Kris looked around the booth. "You may *think*

this is a joke," she said with dignity, "but I assure you, it is *not*."

We all pinched back laughter. Kristie would make a great Marine, I thought. Or corporate executive. Only executives had to wear suits, and it was hard to imagine Kris in pinstripes. She was more of a T-shirt kind of person.

The coffee came. Everyone but me dumped a gallon of cream into their cups. Then we paused to order a pile of food—pancakes, eggs, French toast, you name it. We interrupted each other and changed our orders and shouted to the waitress. Eating out with friends was a riot.

"I'm so nervous," Kris whispered, after the waitress took off again.

"Don't be scared," Janell said, patting her hand. "The food here is bad, but not that bad." Then she laughed until she collapsed over the Formica tabletop.

"I wasn't talking about the food," Kris said, almost shouting over Janell's wild laughter. "I meant I was nervous about meeting Max. Don't forget, I'm the club president. Most of the pressure is on me."

"Before you said that," I told her, "I wasn't nervous at all. Don't talk about it any more or I will be."

Kris clammed up, but her face got pink, as if she were holding her breath.

"My brother said if he heard one more word

about Max Adamms, he was going to croak," Janell added. "I said if he thought I was bad, he should see Kristie."

Kris laughed and curled her hands around Janell's throat.

"My father says I'm obsessed," Chels said, ripping open a sugar packet. She sprinkled some granules delicately into her coffee, stirred, then dumped the rest in and opened another packet. "He says I have Max on the brain. I don't see what's so bad about being obsessed. Dad's an orthodontist, and *he's* obsessed with teeth. He talks about bicuspids and molars all the time."

We were all quiet for awhile. "Obsessed," said Janell. "I don't like the sound of that." She turned to me. "Do you feel obsessed?"

I shrugged. "What are the signs?"

"You lose touch with reality. Have you lost touch with reality?"

"I don't think so."

"I mean, you still eat and sleep and think of other things besides Max Adamms, don't you?"

I thought this over. It wasn't easy to concentrate, because the other members of the fan club were drilling their eyeballs into my skull. But my mind managed to put together an idea. I definitely thought of other things besides Max. Maybe because I have learned that no one person is perfect and you can't pin too much hope on anybody. He or she could really disappoint you. Even people who don't

78

mean to disappoint you—like parents—sometimes can't help it, because they're just human. But God is different. He never lets me down. In fact, He is the only security I really have. I thought about God, and a coffee-like warmth suddenly sloshed through my stomach. It was good to have God on my side—always.

"Yeah," I answered, finally. "I still think of a lot of things besides old Maxie boy."

Janell let out a relieve breath. "I know I do, too. Just this morning I was thinking how my band teacher is going to kill me because I didn't practice my trombone this week. I was too busy reading about Max in the book Kris loaned to me." She looked worried and took a big gulp of her coffee. She made a horrible face and set the cup down.

"Still," said Peg, snickering, "Max is the cutest guy to walk on two feet."

We started to chant together, but not loud enough to disturb our neighbors: "We're not obsessed! We're not obsessed!"

Kris, I noticed, wasn't joining in. She sat looking at her fork, turning it over and over as if it were an amazing piece of art.

The waitress came back, balancing trays of food on her arm. Once the plates were in front of the right people, Chels ordered, "Dig in!"

We did.

13

"Kris is really gone," Chels said, rolling her eyes and impressing me with a long, low whistle. "I'm worried about her."

We were between classes, talking on the stairwell. Kids pushed past us, but we held our ground. Sometimes it's hard to find a secluded place at Keats just to talk. Peter, I noticed, slunk by, a mashed figure in the crowd.

"What about you?" I said. Then, to be fair, I added, "—and me, and all the other members of the club? We're all pretty whipped on Max."

"Listen, kid, this conversation doesn't change the fact that I am still a dependable admirer. It's just that I've got limits. I know when to quit. Kris is different." With her hair pulled back in combs and her face frowning sternly, Chelsie looked like a history teacher giving a serious lecture on the Spanish Armada or something. "We're not freaked out the way Kris is. She's gone."

I looked around nervously. Chelsie was talking at full volume, and if someone from the fan club came by, there'd be trouble. Chelsie sometimes lacks discretion.

"Half of the stuff we read in those magazines is probably made up," she was saying, arching her eyebrows dramatically. "I know what goes on in Hollywood. The studio or his agent or someone says, 'Max, my boy, here's the image you're going to project.' And that's that. His fate is sealed." She looked down at me with satisfaction.

How irritating. It took all the romance out of things to be standing there while someone psycho-analyzed the whole situation. I wanted to push off and yell, "See you at lunch, kiddo." But Chels had a grip on my arm.

"—And anyway, how can we really get to know him from a couple of publicity pictures and a TV sitcom?"

"I'm convinced," I said, though I wasn't sure I was. "What are you going to do about Kristie?"

Her shoulders drooped. "Nothing, I guess. Just wait it out." She drew a breath and suddenly looked around as if she were surprised to find herself in the middle of her own junior high school. "Oh, look," she said. "Here he comes again, Vic."

Peter was thumping down the stairs. Chels waited until he was just across from us, and then she gave me a little push in his direction. I stumbled and knocked into his shoulder. Embarrassing. Also fairly dangerous. If I hadn't been weak from mortification, I would have been furious at Chels. But she had taken off.

"Sorry about that," I said to Peter. I was glad the traffic had thinned out; there hadn't been an audience for that last stunt. Or this conversation.

"That's okay," he said.

"*Friends*," I said, rolling my eyes.

"Yeah," he said. "Friends." He paused. "Hey, did you get my message? I called you a couple of nights ago."

I whapped my forehead. "I forgot to call! I got home too late and—"

"That's okay," he said hurriedly, looking at the bottom steps like he wanted to make a quick escape. "I didn't call for any big deal. Just, sort of, to talk."

I didn't know what to say. I had heard of guys doing that, but it had not actually happened to me. My hands got unexpectedly clammy, and I started staring at that bottom step, too. There was a smashed wad of pink gum on the edge. Don't ask me why I had this reaction. Peter was, as I have said before, just a friend. We had stuff in common. So I don't know why I was making it such a big deal.

"Well," he said, "I gotta go to class." Every

conversation at school seemed to end this way.

"Yeah, me too," I said. "Maybe I'll give you a call or something."

"Okay."

"Bye."

"Bye."

I zombied off to class, thinking I must be losing my marbles. These days, problems seemed to come zooming out of nowhere, without a clue. Maybe I was finally entering what I had heard adults refer to as "troubled adolescence." I hoped not.

By the time school was over for the day, I knew what I had to do. I had thought about it and reconsidered and talked myself back into it. But first, I had to get home.

Chels walked with me. Usually I didn't mind taking it slow, but tonight I could hardly keep myself from running. I didn't want to make her suspicious, however, so I trudged along, occasionally stopping to wad together a quick snowball to throw at her.

"Well," she said at the gate to my place, "another boring day." For a second I was afraid she'd want to come inside, but she just waved at me cheerfully. "Tally-ho."

For secrecy's sake, I went around back. *What a great sleuth I'd make*, I thought, unlocking the door. I'm naturally sneaky. "Mo-o-m?" I yelled, though I knew she wouldn't be home until much later. And Matthew was still at the neighbors' house. The Johnstons kept him out of trouble until I got home. Without even pulling off my coat, I flipped on the radio and tuned it to the familiar station. Yep, Dr. Airhart was on, murmuring "Hmmm," while some lady talked about being lonely. My heart was pounding. I had to turn up the radio so I could hear.

It was now or never. I went to the phone and dialed the number, which I had memorized. It rang.

"Talk line," a woman's voice answered. "May I help you?"

"Doc—Doctor Airhart?"

"No, this is the receptionist. If you'll give me your name, I'll put you on hold until the doctor is free to talk with you."

I gave her my name.

"Do you have a problem to talk over with Dr. Airhart?"

"Yes. I mean, sort of. Actually, it's more of a question than a problem."

For a second I thought she might make me tell her what it was. Telling it once was going to be tough. But twice, and to a total stranger, was terrible. She didn't ask any more questions. She just said, "Hold on a second, and Dr. Airhart will put you on the air."

I waited a whole lifetime. I kept hearing noises, like the back door opening. Just what I needed—my family coming in while I was relating my most personal, private problems. While I waited, music played and the second hand on the kitchen clock went around. I tried to think how I would phrase my question.

Suddenly there was a click in my ear and a familiar gravelly voice said, "This is Dr. Airhart. You're on the air."

My mind was totally numb. I was speechless.

"Hello?" said the voice.

"Hi," I croaked out.

"This is Dr. Airhart," she repeated. "You're on the air."

"I—I think I have a problem."

"Uh-huh," she said and paused. "Why don't you tell me about it?"

I swallowed. "Today I had a very strange experience," I said. "But really it's been going on for a long time. Maybe I should go back to the beginning."

"That would be a good idea."

"I have these friends, four of them, who are wild about this TV star. Should I tell you what his name is?"

"That's not necessary."

"And we've been gearing up to go meet him. He'll be in town this Saturday. So everyone can hardly wait."

"Hmmm."

"At first I didn't know if I sort of liked him a little or if I was in love with him." Even saying this over

85

the phone I couldn't help blushing. Luckily she couldn't see that. But, being a psychiatrist and all, she could probably *sense* it. I rushed on with my story. "A friend of mine says all of the magazine articles are just a bunch of hype anyway, not real facts, but, I mean, I'm still pretty thrilled to go meet him. Then there's this real guy—I mean a guy I go to school with—who called me up, just to talk, and even though I know he's just a friend, I was sort of, you know, nervous about it, and hyped up. You know?"

"Sure," she said.

"And I was just wondering. Is this halfway . . . normal or . . . ?" My voice trailed off. I was out of breath.

The doctor paused. From listening to her show, I knew she never rushed into her advice. So I gave her time to think and didn't worry. I just held onto the receiver, hearing my own heart pound in my ear.

"How old are you?" Dr. Airhart asked after a moment.

"I'm . . ." My mind blinked out again. Then came back. "Thirteen. And a half."

"Well," she said. "Your situation sounds very normal. But you probably feel like a great human yo-yo, huh?"

I smiled. "Sort of."

"Listen, things are going to be confusing for awhile. Don't worry."

"So what do I do while things are confusing?"

"Just wait and see."

"But—" I sputtered, no words coming out. "It's so confusing and—"

"Hmm," said Dr. Airhart kindly. "Life *is* confusing, isn't it?"

I couldn't believe it. I had called the expert and she didn't have the answers. Like all adults, she wanted me to "wait and see."

The doctor's voice came through the phone. "Can you talk to your mom and dad when things get jumbled up?"

My mind pictured their faces. "Yeah," I said into the receiver. "They're great. They wouldn't make fun or do anything insensitive."

"Good. Don't be afraid to ask for their help."

"Okay," I said. I waited for her to sign off. But she paused again.

"Do you . . . like this other boy? Romantically?"

For about the millionth time in my life, I considered it. Finally I said, "Nope. We're friends. I like Peter as a friend."

Then I realized what I had done. *Oh no!* I moaned silently. I had said his name on the air!

"Well, that's fine, then. Just relax and try to enjoy things. Okay? Thanks for calling."

After I had hung up, I kept my hands over my eyes for about five minutes, wishing I could just crawl into a dark place forever. If anyone found out about this I was sunk. Cooked. Finished.

14

In the car on Saturday, no one made a peep. Not one sound. Our mouths were clamped shut. We just sat there, clutching our posters and books on our laps.

Every few minutes, Chels or Peg turned around and gave us back-seat riders a wink. Today was the day. Max Adamms was in town.

Dad gripped the wheel, checking our faces in the rear view mirror. For the first few miles he had chattered away, business as usual, but now he was quiet, too. I think he'd never seen us silent before. We were only a few miles from the mall, and every inch that we drove brought us closer to a real TV star . . . closer to Max Adamms.

Finally Dad couldn't stand it anymore. "It's so quiet in here, my ears are ringing," he said. "Is my driving that terrifying?"

That got us laughing. Laughing helped loosen the knot in my stomach.

"We're just nervous," said Chels.

"I'm the most nervous," said Kristie. "I'm president of the club. I'll have to introduce you guys. How am I supposed to talk to a celebrity when I'm scared out of my gourd?"

Dad thought the question over seriously. "Just think of him as a normal guy. Pretend you go to school with him."

We exchanged more looks. Dad didn't understand. Max Adamms, a normal guy? Impossible.

"We're here," announced Peggy, bouncing on the seat. "Do I look okay, you guys?"

Janell squinted at her. "Next to my awesome beauty, you look . . . adequate."

I bounded from the car. "See you, Dad," I said.

"Wait a second."

I leaned back in the window as everyone climbed out of the car.

"You still want me to give you all a ride home?"

"Of course. Could you check the bookstore in an hour? We should be done by then."

"Will do."

"Unless," Chels added, "Max wants us to go to a special party in his honor or something." She paused. "Just kidding."

Dad revved the motor a little. "I'll do some shopping, then I'll locate you guys. Have fun." He pulled away.

"Have fun, he says," said Kristie.

I pointed to the mall entrance. "Let's go."

We pulled open the glass doors and entered the warm mall.

Even before we turned the corner toward the store we could hear the hoopla. The line stretched past the eyeglasses store and the trick shop. It reached all the way to the fountain. Everyone was our age, I noticed. We quickly grabbed our spots and stood fidgeting.

"What'll I say to him?" Kristie asked. "For the first time, I'm sorry I am president of the club."

Janell gave her a poke. "Get hold of yourself, Kris, old girl. You're making *me* nervous. Just think about what Mr. Mahoney said and be yourself."

"I can't," she moaned.

Right then I said a prayer, not only for me, but for Kristie, too. She looked terrible. Maybe people would think it was funny to pray about something like that, but it was nice to have Someone to turn to, no matter how unusual the occasion.

"Somebody should go to the front of the line to see if he's here, yet," Chels said, taking charge. "I'll do it."

Before any of us could object, she jogged away, wearing her determined look. We couldn't have stopped her if we'd thrown our bodies in her path.

90

We craned our necks, watching until she disappeared.

In a few moments she was back. Even before she opened her mouth, we could tell from her face that Max wasn't here yet.

"No go," she announced. "There's a table set up and some burly security guards around, but no Max in sight. While we wait, let's do inventory. Kris, do you have the book?"

Kristie pulled the big picture book out of a crinkled paper bag. "Check."

"Pen?"

She held one up. "Check."

Chels was satisfied. "I guess we're all set, then. There's nothing to do but wait."

"Look at all these *girls*," Peg said. "Max sure has a lot of fans."

"Hey!" shouted Chels. "The line is moving!"

Sure enough, we had to take a few steps to catch up with the girls ahead of us (who were, I noticed, dressed to the hilt in new jeans, expensive sweaters, and exotic jewelry). I looked down at my old Levis and slightly faded pullover. Gross.

"He must be here," Chels said to Kristie, giving her a little push. "Go see."

Kris just looked at her blankly. "Me?"

"Go on, kiddo. You're the president."

She left, dragging her feet. We waited for her to reappear.

"At the rate she was moving, we'll probably get

there before she does," Janell said, putting her hands on her hips.

Finally we saw her. She was running, and her Max Adamms for President T-shirt billowed behind her like a parachute. Her face looked as though it might burst with excitement.

"He's here!"

We clustered around and waited for her to catch her breath. "He's wearing a turquoise sweater and jeans," she said. "I couldn't really see much else because the security guards are really grouchy. One of 'em said, 'Stand back, miss,' like I was going to attack him or something. They wouldn't let me get too close. He's started signing books. Can you stand it? It's too exciting!"

She was back to her old self.

After that, the line moved pretty quickly. They must have been shuttling the fans through like cattle. I hoped I looked okay. The last thing you want is to look grungy when you meet a famous TV actor.

Now we were close enough to see his head moving as he took a book from someone, looked up at the person, and then leaned over to sign the book. If I had to sign my name that many times my penmanship would fall apart.

"Only five more people ahead of us," Chelsie whispered. "What am I gonna say?"

"Kris is the one with the book," I reminded her. "She's going to introduce us, remember?"

"I'll try to keep my mouth shut," Chelsie promised, "but in pressured situations like this, I can't always be responsible for my actions. Get ready for anything."

"Okay," I agreed.

Max was signing the book of the girl ahead of us. He finished signing, closed the book, and handed it up to the girl. "Thanks, Max, thanks so much, you don't know how much I appreciate this," she gushed. The guard motioned her along, we all leaned forward, and suddenly Max looked right up at Kristie.

"H-hi, Max," she said.

He looked smaller than he did on TV. Skinnier. But he looked up and flashed his all-famous smile, and that gave Kris the courage to go on.

"These are the members of our . . . your . . . fan club," she said, extending her arm. The way she pointed at us reminded me of the way people on commercials point at appliances.

Meanwhile Max plucked the book right out of her arms and started scribbling. "Thanks for your support," he said. "I really appreciate it." Then he snapped the book shut and handed it to her. He reached for the poster Chelsie was holding.

"Uh," continued Kristie, "the names of the club members are Peggy Hiltshire, Janell Hornsby, Vick—"

"Thanks for your support," Max said to Chelsie and grabbed my poster.

"And I'm the president of the club," Kris said,

desperately pointing a finger at herself.

By now the whole group had their posters signed, and the guard gave us the quick motion out of the line. It was over.

We stood there in a circle, sort of dazed. Kris looked like she had just been punched.

"*That* was quick," said Peggy.

We looked over our shoulders at Max. His head was bent and he was busy signing away.

"I can't believe it," said Kristie, turning back toward the fountain. "I hardly even got a look at him."

"I think he's cuter in person than he is on TV," Chelsie announced. "What did you think?"

"I think he bites his fingernails," said Janell. "Did you take a look at them? They were bitten down to the nubs."

"Let's see his handwriting," Peg said, grabbing the book from Kris's limp hands. "You can tell a lot about someone by his handwriting."

The signature started with a lump of an M, followed by an almost straight line, and a lump of an A, followed by another almost straight line.

Chelsie giggled. "If you can tell a lot about a person by his handwriting, I'd say Max Adamms is an S-L-O-B, slob."

"He needs to practice his penmanship," I said. "He'd never make it in Keats Junior High."

Chelsie suddenly turned to Kristie. "Hey, Madam President, you never said my name. I kept waiting for my big moment to be introduced."

"He didn't *let* me. I tried, and he cut me off."

Chels crossed her arms and was silent.

"She did try," I agreed.

Peg cut in. "I don't think he was trying to be rude," she said. "He was just in a hurry."

Janell shook her head so her earrings jangled. "Even if he was in a big fat hurry, he could have said, 'Well, howdy there, Kristie-Baby. Thanks for heading up this little fan club, instead of"—and she stared into space, bug-eyed, like a robot—" 'Thank-you-for-your-support.' " She scowled. "It was the security guards' fault. They zapped us out of the line so fast, my head is still spinning."

Suddenly it hit us. Our big event was over. It was like Christmas, when all that's left are the crumpled piles of wrapping paper. We stood gripping our posters, just five pathetic faces in a mob of Max Adamms fans.

Suddenly a familiar voice behind us called, "Hello, hello!"

I swiveled around. Dad strode cheerfully toward us with a grin on his face. Suddenly I had a funny feeling, something I hadn't felt since being a kid: I remembered how it felt to see my parents again after I'd spent an afternoon with a baby-sitter. I had the urge to rush over and wrap my arms around him and say, "I'm so glad you're back!" Fortunately I restrained myself.

"Well?" he asked. "How'd it go? Did you catch a

glimpse of the adored Mr. Adamms?"

Everyone just looked at him dully.

"Uh-oh," he said. "I thought you'd be able to talk again *after* you saw him; you couldn't *before*."

"Let's just say," I told him, "that the whole thing was an experience. Let's hit the road."

"At your service," he said with a bow.

"Wait, wait!" said Peg. "Can you just make one teeny-weeny detour through the dime store? I want to see if any of the new magazines are out."

While the others nosed around the magazines, I headed for the posters. There were huge shots of every TV star ever born, including Max in a thousand different poses.

Then I saw a face that made me stop. Under the heading "Historical Figures" I had found my brother's dream poster: a photograph of Eleanor Roosevelt's smiling face. I pulled one out of the rack. *On second thought*, I decided, *make that one for Matthew, one for me*. Grinning, with the rolled-up posters stashed under my arm, I went back to find my friends. They'd never believe this.

15

I stood outside the family room. Yep, everyone was in there. Dad was doing sit-ups and groaning like he was about to die. Mom was holding his feet. Matthew was fiddling with the knobs of the stereo. The volume of the exercise album was turned to "deafening."

"And now—!" I shouted into the room to get their attention.

They all jumped and turned toward the door.

"—the star of the show, the girl of the forties, may I present to you, Victoria Hope Mahoney!"

I ran in and fell on one knee. Luckily, I didn't hear any ripping sounds from my black maid's dress. I held the position, my foot wobbling a little in the black high heels with rhinestone buckles. Mom, Dad, and Matthew just stared at me, stunned.

"Well?" I said. "How do I look?"

"Semi-glamorous," Mom said, finally.

"Why only semi?"

"Your hair is coming undone. On the left side."

I put my hand up. Rats. My sausage curls were already starting to droop. Maybe I still had time to go fire up the curling iron again before Grandpa Harold came to pick me up.

My brother made a face. "What's all that red gunk on your mouth?"

"Lipstick," I said. "For Pete's sake, you've seen lipstick before. A lot of women in the forties wore it—especially bright red. Eleanor Roosevelt probably did."

Matthew yawned. "I'm tired of Eleanor Roosevelt."

I let my jaw drop to the floor. "What?! After I bought you that poster?"

"She's okay," he said. "But now I like cars." He drove a miniature car up the side of the couch, making loud engine noises.

Good grief. Little kids are so fickle.

Dad sat up and curled his arms around his knees. "You look very authentic, Vickie," he said.

Mom nodded. "I agree. Not that I remember what people in the forties looked like. That was a little before my time." She gave Dad a wicked slice of a smile.

Just as Dad was ready to lunge at her, the doorbell rang. Probably Grandpa Harold.

"Well," I said, standing up carefully. "Guess I have to go, now—drooping curls and all. See you cats later." I flashed them the two-fingered "V" for victory sign. This, I had heard, was very common during World War II.

"I have just made an interesting discovery," I said to Isadora. We were pressed against the kitchen counter, working on hors d' oeurves together.

"No fooling," she said. "What's that?"

"That it is very difficult to make Swedish meat-balls with false fingernails on." I held up my hands. There was a long red fingernail missing from each.

"Good grief," said Isadora. "Where'd they go?"

I giggled and pointed into the mixing bowl, which was filled with raw hamburger. "In there."

"Well, that's very funny, Victoria, but make sure both of those fingernails are accounted for before you put the meatballs in the oven."

"The hamburger keeps getting wedged under my nails. Ick."

"I used to have red claws a mile long, just like that. What a nuisance. I like mine short and functional now."

My nails were short and functional, too; I never could grow them any longer than about one-tenth of an inch.

Grandpa Harold came into the kitchen.

"Eccchh," he said, looking into the bowl.

"It'll be delicious," I said, putting one found fingernail on the counter. "You want your old college buds to be impressed, don't you?"

"Once they meet my charming granddaughter, they'll fall over in amazement."

He pressed his cheek against mine, and then he took off again. He was wearing an old letterman's jacket and a ton of cologne. The cologne didn't cover the smell of mothballs, and the jacket wouldn't have buttoned over his stomach in a million years, but he looked highly romantic. The way Isadora was looking at him, she must have thought so, too. Come to think of it, she looked pretty snazzy, herself. She was wearing this crazy wig (snood and all), and shoulder pads about six miles high. I was padded up to my eyeballs, too.

"By the way," Iz said after a while, "how did that star business at the mall go last weekend?"

"Well—" I said, "it sort of happened fast. Max didn't have much time to spend with us, and I think he hurt my friend Kristie's feelings. She's sort of sensitive. She was *living* for the moment when she'd see old Max."

Isadora flashed a look at me. "What're you going to do now? Dump Max? Pull out of the fan club?"

I shook my head no. His picture was still on my wall, but I had moved it to make room for Eleanor's. I like Eleanor hanging over my desk. I could look up at her for inspiration. I had even borrowed some of Matthew's library books about her—to find out what made her tick.

"Don't worry about your friend," Isadora said, spooning herring into a dish. (Herring makes me queasy, but I didn't say that to Isadora. After all, I was the maid, not the guest.) "I bet she'll get over her disappointment. Life goes on."

That was true.

"You know," she continued, putting a mound of potatoes in front of me, and placing a vegetable peeler in my hand, "I have a celebrity friend of my own."

"Really?" I asked. "Who?"

"An old college roommate. Smart as a whip. I invited her specially, and she's coming."

"Who is she?"

"Ginger Rogers."

I dropped the peeler and stared at Isadora, who gaffawed and slapped my back.

"Goodness, granddaughter, you're gullible. Just kidding! Actually my friend is a local radio personality, someone you've probably never heard of: Angela Airhart."

You don't realize how small an apartment is until you try to entertain two dozen of your grandparents' ex-college friends in it. The doorbell kept ringing and ringing, and Isadora or Harold kept swinging open the door and letting more people in. The clothes on these people were wild. There were skirt and sweater sets, bobby socks and loafers. There were letter sweaters, dapper suits, gloves and big shoulder pads. And, of course, the smell of mothballs. Some people wore hats. The men took theirs off as they ducked through the doorway. The women kept theirs on, and the veils covered their eyes like elegant cobwebs. I'd never seen anything like it.

I piled food on my tray and snaked through the room. "May I offer you an hors d' oeurve?" I asked, adding just a hint of an English accent for elegance. The meatballs disappeared by the truckload.

Nervously I kept my eyes pealed for Dr. Airhart, but there wasn't one plump, white-haired woman in the vicinity. That was a relief. Maybe she wouldn't show. Maybe someone had called for emergency advice and she had been detained.

Guiltily, I hoped so. The last thing I needed was to run into a psychiatrist who knew all of my deepest secrets. Dr. Airhart was sharp. She'd recognize my voice in a second. "Ohhh," she'd say, "You're the silly girl with the crush on the TV star. And didn't you mention a specific boy . . . let's see . . . a Peter someone?" Arrgh.

After awhile I started to relax. The bell had stopped ringing. The guests were having the time of their lives. And the place smelled wonderful— spiced cider, coffee, warm pumpkin pie. Even Isadora's herring smelled festive. I circled the room while Bing Crosby crooned his heart out on the stereo, and people told joke after joke. They sure were a jolly group. They made as much noise as my friends and I did when we were together.

Isadora caught my arm as I rushed by with my tray.

"Victoria, look at this." She was pointing to the legs of a woman whose back was turned to me.

"Look at what?" I asked, staring at the woman's legs.

"Look!" she said pointing. "See those dark seam lines? During the war, silk stockings were so scarce, we used to draw seams on our legs to look like real stockings. Angela, here, had the steadiest hand in the dorm."

"Oh," I said, smiling politely. Then I sucked in a quick breath. *Angela?*

Too late. The woman turned around. Dr. Angela Airhart.

Isadora was beaming. "Angela, I'd like you to meet my granddaughter, Victoria Mahoney. Vickie, this is the celebrity I was telling you about—Dr. Angela Airhart."

The doc reached out and took my hand to shake. "Victoria. It's so nice to meet you."

"Hello," I said, shaking her hand and looking up at her.

She was taller, even taller than Isadora. Her hair was long, to her shoulder, and swept off to the side. It wasn't any one color—more like a combination of blonde, soft brown, and gray. She was beautiful. The half-moon glasses and the white lab coat I had

103

imagined were nowhere in sight.

"I've heard your show," I said. "In fact, I listen to it a lot."

She smiled, and I noticed that her two front teeth overlapped. I liked that.

"I'm told a lot of kids your age tune in. I guess everyone could use a little advice now and again."

Maybe later, I thought, I could subtly bring up the subject of Kristie, who had been down ever since last weekend. Maybe the doctor had seen this problem before. She might even have some practical advice. I could just imagine her leaning against the kitchen cupboards and saying "Hmmm" while she slowly sipped apple cider and nodded her head.

16

At church the next morning, the last traces of Christmas had vanished.

A crew of volunteers must have moved through with boxes and vacuum cleaners. The banners were gone. The Advent candles were gone. The place was back to its old self.

But the vestibule was bright with light as the four of us, Mom, Dad, Matthew, and I walked in. There were clumps of people standing around and talking a mile a minute. The smell of coffee was in the air, and I had this nice feeling that I had just arrived at a big party. I was glad to be there.

My church is in an old building in the middle of a neighborhood. The floor creaks. The light fixtures are fuzzy with dust. When you lean back in a pew, the wood sometimes gives a long "craaackkk" like it's going to split apart.

We headed toward the sanctuary, but we had to step aside to let Mattie Baker pass. I hadn't seen her since that day in the sports store. She was herding a pack of tiny kids out after their rehearsal, and her arms were stretched out like a mother robin's.

"Stay together, little birds," she called to them. "Stay together."

Then she glanced up and saw our whole Mahoney gang standing there. Her crew cut glittered as the sun slanted through the sanctuary windows, and she grinned. Mattie has enormous teeth, all dazzlers.

"Some days," she said, "these guys drive me right to the brink. You know? There are times when I'd like to tear my hair out—if I had any!" She laughed and we laughed, and finally she got them corralled, out the door, and down the stairs to the Sunday school rooms.

Matthew picked out a perfect pew for us. (No surprise there, since he picks the same pew every Sunday.) We settled in.

Chels came slinking up the aisle. "Hi," she whispered, crashing in next to me. "I almost didn't make it. I thought I'd lost my favorite black shoes. Finally I found them—on the shoe rack in my closet. Of all places. Now I can't find the book Kristie loaned me. If I've lost that book, Kris will do something drastic, I just know it."

106

Vaguely, I wondered what old Max Adamms was doing. Flying to a book signing? Reading about himself in the latest *Teen Fan* magazine?

A guy from Sunday school walked past us on his way down the aisle, and Chels cut the chatter abruptly. She was all eyes. I had noticed that Chelsie dropped Max Adamms like a hot potato whenever a real guy walked by. I had forgotten to ask Dr. Angie to explain *that*.

Dad was giving me a look, so I nudged Chelsie. We sat up straight. Before the service, Mom and Dad like us to sit quietly and sort of meditate and pray and stuff. I forced my mind back into a concentration mode.

Things got underway. The music director led a song and we sat down. Then he announced that Mattie and the Songbirds would present the special music.

Now the whole noisy gang of them were trooping down the aisle. The Songbirds waved at the people they knew in the audience. At last Mattie got them all clustered in rows on the steps.

"Hit it!" she said to the pianist, and the piano crashed into the song.

It was a piece every church kid knows: "Oh, I've got joy, joy, joy, joy, down in my heart!" Those kids screamed the words, all on different notes. I could practically see down to their tonsils. Mom gave me a nudge in the ribs and a sideways smile. "Remember when you performed that song?" she whispered.

107

Yeah. A long time ago, as a Songbird, I had tripped down the aisle in my choir robe, too. I had waited for Mattie to pack me into the front row (that's where they put you when you're short) and hoped that she wouldn't make me stand next to any boys.

Things had changed. I had changed.

"—joy, joy, joy, joy, down in my heart!"

For instance, now I understood the song. Joy was something "down in my heart" that never went away. Even without all the decorations and the special Advent celebrations, the whole year was a holiday if you believed in the Lord. For a Christian, there was always a reason to celebrate, no matter what the circumstances.

I sat back, stunned by this sudden discovery. Joy wasn't a giggling-all-the-time kind of honey-sweetness. It was something deeper. It was why I didn't lose hope, even when I'd been disappointed. It was why Mattie, who had a scary disease, still smiled. Probably it was the sort of mysterious thing that Dr. Airhart knew nothing about.

On the third verse, Mattie turned around and motioned to the congregation. Her arms flapped like a bird's, and her robe made a great fabricky racket.

I joined in, belting out the song at the top of my lungs.

JUST VICTORIA

I am absolutely *dreading* junior high.

Vic and her best friend, Chelsie, have heard enough gory details about seventh grade to ruin their entire summer vacation. And as if school weren't a big enough worry, Vic suddenly finds problems at every turn:

• Chelsie starts hanging around Peggy Hiltshire, queen of all the right cliques, who thinks life revolves around the cheerleading squad.

• Vic's mom gets a "fulfilling" new job—with significantly less pay—at a nursing home.

• Grandma Warden is looking tired and pale—and won't see a doctor.

But Victoria Hope Mahoney has a habit of underestimating her own potential. The summer brings a lot of change, but Vic is equal to it as she learns more about her faith, friendship, and growing up.

Don't miss any books in The Victoria Mahoney Series!

Just Victoria · Only Kidding, Victoria

More Victoria · Maybe It's Love, Victoria

Take a Bow, Victoria · Autograph, Please, Victoria

SHELLY NIELSEN lives in Minneapolis, Minnesota, with her husband and two Yorkshire terriers.

ONLY KIDDING, VICTORIA

You've got to be kidding!

Spend the summer at a resort lodge in Minnesota . . . with her *family?* When she's been looking forward to endless days of good times with her new friends from school?

Victoria can't believe her parents are serious, but nothing she can do or say will change their minds. It's off to Little Raccoon Lake, a nowhere place where she's sure there will be nothing to do.

But the summer holds a lot of surprises—like Nina, one year older and a whole lot tougher, who scoffs at rules . . . and at Vic for bothering to keep them. And the bittersweet pang that comes with each letter from her best friend, Chelsie, reminding Vic of what she's missing back home. But the biggest surprise is Victoria's discovery of some things that have been right under her nose all along . . . .

Don't miss any books in
The Victoria Mahoney Series!

Just Victoria	Only Kidding, Victoria
More Victoria	Maybe It's Love, Victoria
Take a Bow, Victoria	Autograph, Please, Victoria

SHELLY NIELSEN lives in Minneapolis, Minnesota, with her husband and two Yorkshire terriers.

HERE COMES GINGER!

God, stop Mom's wedding!

Ginger's world is falling apart. Her mom has recently become a Christian and, even worse, has fallen in love with Grant Gabriel. Ginger can't stand the thought of leaving their little house near the beach . . . moving in with Grant and his two children . . . trading in her "brown cave of a bedroom" for a yellow canopied bed.

Ginger tries to fight the changes she knows are coming—green fingernails, salt in the sugar bowl, a near disaster at the beach. But she finds that change can happen inside her, too, when she meets the Lord her mom has come to trust.

The Ginger Series
   Here Comes Ginger!   A Job for an Angel
   Off to a New Start   Absolutely Green

ELAINE L. SCHULTE is a southern Californian, like Ginger. She has written many stories, articles, and books for all ages, but the **Ginger Trumbell Books** is her first series for kids.

Chariot Books™
David C. Cook Publishing Co.

OFF TO A NEW START

Aoooouuuuh!
Aooooouuuuuh!

The blast of Ginger's conch shell sounds through the Gabriels' house. But is it a call to battle or a plea for peace?

Some days Ginger isn't sure, as she struggles to find her place in her new "combined" family, in her new school, and as a new child of God. With the wise counsel of Grandfather Gabriel and the support of her family, Ginger learns some important lessons about making friends and making peace.

The Ginger Series
>   Here Comes Ginger!   A Job for an Angel
>   Off to a New Start   Absolutely Green

ELAINE L. SCHULTE is a southern Californian, like Ginger. She has written many stories, articles, and books for all ages, but the **Ginger Trumbell Books** is her first series for kids.

Chariot Books ™
David C. Cook Publishing Co.